GOING NOWHERE SLOW

AUSTIN HAWKINS

AMARANTH

Defiant Books. Timeless Ideas.

For Sam

CHAPTER ONE

EVERY FALL, GROUPS OF WIDE-EYED MIDWESTERN YOUTH stumbled over each other as they searched for their morning classes. The buildings stood identical in both structure and stature, and to add to the confusion, in 1998, Baxter State College removed all gaudy signage that had clear names for the buildings for more tasteful plaques placed near the entryways. This was, of course, due to the Great Helvetica Scandal of 1996, the new plaques intended to preemptively squash future riots. As a state-funded school, the kids who chose to attend Baxter State College were oftentimes challenged in both comprehension and reading abilities. They'd stand outside each building and carefully inspect their class schedules before looking back toward the building, slack-jawed and empty-headed. The students stood for hours as they attempted to decipher where they stood in relation to the building, where they thought they ought to be, and the address in their outheld hands. There seemed to exist a strange ether between the address, the student, and the building, obscuring one from the other.

Thurston Ford threaded through the throngs of mindless youth without much thought. His shoulders slumped from hours of bent-over research, which was how he referred to the nights spent commenting on obscure internet forums. Due to his unnatural curvature, clothes loosely draped him like a cloak. His shirt hung over his small gut. Slight pimples lined his brow line, which he exacerbated by constant picking and popping. His hair curled and hung in front of his eyes. With his back straightened and a healthy tan, Thurston could have been a decent-looking fellow; however, his sullen and sunken look only attracted the spookiest of women.

For Thurston, devilish women were still women, as far he could tell. Their makeup was darker, and their taste in music scared him, but all the bits and pieces of a relationship seemed to be about the same: coffee dates and a string of broken promises until the inevitable breakup. That was until Martha.

Martha Pendergrift entered Thurston's life like an explosion. She worked at the coffee shop near campus, and Thurston admired her from a distance. She was his type, or at least she was the type that typically found him attractive, and that was all it took. Thurston really only liked women who liked him first. She was small and dangerously spooky. A spider web tattoo crawled down her arm. Her eyes and hair were jet black, and she wore them pulled back in curly, loose braids. One day, as she took his order, she asked him, "What's your problem?"

"Uh, I... nothing?"

Martha leaned over the counter and laughed. "I'm fucking with you, relax. Come see my band. Or don't. Either way."

"Oh, yeah. Of course." Thurston forced a smile.

"See you there. Or not." She said and handed him his coffee. Her loose braids bobbed back and forth with each syllable.

Thurston obliged and later found himself alone in a dingy

punk bar. And despite the visceral fear he felt at the string of obscene, women's health-related songs Martha played, he tapped his foot along, sipped at a warm PBR, and enjoyed himself. After the show, she approached him at the bar and asked, "What did you think?"

"Uh," Thurston said. "Great music. You were great." He lied.

Without another word, she grabbed and kissed him. Thurston didn't realize, but at that exact moment, his life would be measured Before and After Martha, and the After Martha time would be defined by her filling up most aspects of his life. Decisions that he thought were his alone were no longer. She quickly corrected him of that habit, and Thurston came to learn that all decisions needed her consultation.

Eventually, Thurston's grades plummeted. Although never studious, he prided himself on being average, and Martha distracted him enough that he did not even succeed at that. He sat her down on the steps in front of the student center and gingerly explained that they were on different life paths. She cried and said that she understood, but somehow, a month later, she moved into his apartment.

Thurston blanked on how the breakup led to their cohabitation, but he carried the boxes up the stairs and into his small one-bedroom. Each box was filled with duplicate kitchenware and piles upon piles of clothes that had no discernible differences. Fashion escaped him, and Martha was sure to point that out. Every one of his favorite t-shirts was worn and filled with holes and lay tattered upon his body.

The entire relationship felt like a tilt-a-whirl, and Thurston had never been a fan of tilt-a-whirls. The wait in line, feeling dizzy and ill, and everyone around him pointing to her and explaining how fun she must be and how lovely it was that he was along for the ride. But all he wanted was to be off and placed on solid ground.

In class, the professor, Dr. Stanton, droned. The burdensome reality of college for Thurston was the academia of it all. Anions and bonds and energy lulled him to sleep. The thought of paying attention felt unbearable, and the best he could do was physically be in the room.

Although his physical presence did little to help him succeed. He spent most lectures barely alive as he doodled cartoon fish across his notebook; he existed in a delicate balance between sleep and a frightful wakefulness.

"And that is best described as what Mr. Ford?" Dr. Stanton asked. The classroom turned to face him. The pimple-popping, high school valedictorians snickered as Thurston jolted at the sound of his name.

"Of course. The answer is cation." Thurston said. He slumped back down into his chair and continued on his newest drawing. He wrote the words Pilgrim Fish above his latest cartoon, a small guppy adorned with a buckled hat and shoes.

"Mr. Ford. It's pronounced cat-ion. Not like nation. Let's focus, everyone." Dr. Stanton said and pointed toward a list of vocabulary words.

After class, a curvy, bright-colored polo with blonde hair approached Thurston. "We meet once a week in the library and study if you want to join us." She smiled and held out her hand to greet the boy.

A sneer formed across his face, and Thurston laughed it away. "Oh, no. Today was just a fluke. I have plenty of time to study on my own. Thanks for thinking of me." He placed his fish drawing notebook in his bag before calling back to the girl. "You know you guys can use my notecards if you need help studying."

"Oh, wow. That's very nice of you." She said back. Even

with the distance, Thurston could make out the look of disdain as it spread across her face.

The problem for Thurston was that he had yet to realize that he was a mediocre mind trapped within a mediocre body. Life for him hadn't unveiled that secret yet. His lack of self-awareness meant that paying attention only happened occasionally and studying less so.

As Thurston shuffled his way home through the freshman wanderers and the prep school posers, he thought about the blonde in the too-tight orange polo. He had never noticed her before, but now he couldn't stop thinking about her asking him to study. If he needed to study, then he was sure the professor would tell him to study. He stopped, picked up a stone, and hurled it out of frustration. The rock ricocheted off a signpost and returned back to him, hitting Thurston squarely in the shin.

Thurston limped home, every step sending a dull ache up his leg. The sky was a bruised shade of purple, threatening rain, and the wind cut through his thin jacket like a knife. He kept his head down as he crossed the railroad tracks, the sharp clatter of an approaching train making him wince. The fence around his building loomed ahead, as pointless as the extra block it forced him to walk. When he first moved into the apartment, he hurdled the barrier fence and saved two or three precious minutes on his commute. However, all it took was one time of not quite hurdling the fence and a pair of ripped jeans for Thurston to decide that the extra two minutes really didn't hurt him.

From the parking lot, he heard the wail of a new song being written. A soft strum of a C chord followed by the guttural screeching of a dying cat. Thurston had a similar reaction to all of Martha's new music, a swift bodily reaction that came from the gut and nearly always wanted to expel through his mouth.

When he reached the door, the music quieted, and he anticipated a rush of kisses or yelling and prepared himself for both. He held his breath in anticipation as the door opened a creak and revealed Martha cross-legged on the floor with an acoustic guitar across her lap. She struck it spastically like a chicken trying to find the last bits of corn on the ground. Her voice was a low whisper, as she hoped to evoke a huskiness that she didn't readily possess. Much to Thurston's surprise, her drummer, shirtless behind her, gently kissed her neck.

"Oh," Thurston muttered and took a step back. The door slammed in his face. When it reopened, the bandmate pulled his shirt on, and Martha stood with her hands in her pockets.

"Hey, man." The drummer said and pushed past Thurston. At the door, he turned and said, "Catch you later, Martha."

She waved a slight goodbye. Thurston's book bag landed on the floor with a thud. His head pounded as he fumbled through the room. He clutched his head as he made his way to the bathroom, flicked on the light, winced, flicked it back off, and blindly searched the cabinet for Tylenol. The intensity and speed of the headache had him convinced that it had actually been caused by a demon.

The Tylenol burned as he chewed them and swallowed. Martha had returned to whisper singing; the guitar again laid across her lap. After a minute, she stopped and turned to Thurston, who clutched his head and whose eyes were held tightly closed. "Are you even going to ask about my new song?" She placed the guitar down beside herself.

"What?" Thurston said and rocked in his chair. The headache reached his inner ear, and the room spun. His eyes worked to adjust, but nothing stayed in focus. His hearing felt like he was next to a train station, and nothing she said made sense.

"My new song. I knew you heard it. I spent all morning

busking so that we would have money to go out this weekend. I was out there for three hours and only made six dollars. Do you know how degrading it is to share your life with the world and for it to respond with only six dollars? I came home and decided to make lunch, a cup of Ramen Noodles," she explained.

Thurston stared at her blankly. The thought of jumping from the balcony crossed his mind, but he doubted that it would result in anything but pain.

"Anyway, it got me thinking about the nature of art and how important it is to make something that lasts. Art is drifting toward online. Shit, life is drifting online. And all of our attention spans are just shot. But to really stand out, I needed to write an ode to the quick-forgetting, constantly consuming world. Something that will last long after I'm gone." She said and struck a chord. She began to sing.

"Ramen noodles, I've felt your warmth,
It filled me up
With a cup.
Ramen noodles, I love you so,
The way you steam
I nearly scream."

She held out the word scream for a beat too long. Her eyes were closed as she strummed the final chord and awaited Thurston's enthusiasm.

After a moment of silence, she assumed Thurston didn't understand. "It's an indictment of the current socioeconomic times. Artists shouldn't have to starve to prove their worth. I want people to hear my song and think, 'My change feeds this poor girl. Ramen is hardly a meal.' What do you think?"

Thurston paused. His shin throbbed, and a neat red bruise sprouted. He rubbed at it, and he thought about telling Martha about how he didn't care about the drummer or the song and that his shin hurt. His shin preoccupation seemed like speech-lessness.

"I only started talking to Brandon because you didn't seem interested anymore," Martha said. She sat the guitar on the floor with a gentle twang. "Your mopey, sensitive, emo guy schtick was hot for a while, but maybe I need more joie de vivre out of the people I surround myself with." She knocked a cigarette out of the box into her hand. It hung from her mouth as she flicked her lighter.

Thurston understood. He nodded deafly and blindly along. It was a combination of the information of the infidelity and his shin that rendered him disabled.

"I'm speechless." Thurston finally said. He reached for his shin and hoped that she would ask him about his day. Martha rolled her eyes. She stood and opened the front door to blow smoke out.

"You know what? I thought I could deal with it. The passiv-ity. The shrugging. The 'whatever-you-want-Martha' thing."

Thurston stared at the floor in silence.

Martha turned back toward him. Her eyes narrowed. "But you... God, Thurston, you never even *try*. You can't even look me in the eye right now."

"I'm... I'm trying—"

"*No*. You're not." She flicked her cigarette out the door. "You don't fight for anything. Not for me. Not for yourself. I need someone who at least gives a shit."

Martha stood and stepped closer. She brushed Thurston's hair back to look him in the eye. "Until something changes, I'll be staying at my brother's."

Without another word, Martha left Thurston alone. She emerged from the bedroom within seconds. The duffel bag had been packed, and she left him to nurse his wounded shin.

CHAPTER TWO

THURSTON'S SHIN ACHED. HE CURSED THE ROCK UNDER his breath and hobbled into the kitchen to pour himself a large glass of milk. The milk cooled his mind and his heartache, but he wished it was ice cream, which always seemed to work a little quicker for grief. He stared out the window to watch Martha prepare to leave.

The duffel bag thudded against each step as she made her way to the car. Martha yelped as she heaved the heavy bag into the trunk and then placed the guitar in the backseat, careful not to hit it on anything. She looked back toward the apartment and waved. Thurston squirmed at the wave and tried to duck, but instead, it looked like he was practicing a sad, wombling salsa. He gave a slight wave back and returned to his chair in the corner.

A sudden and vicious relief overcame Thurston. There was no one to pester or badger or tell him what to do. He could masturbate, he thought, but decided that it may be too soon to fall into carnal desires. And so, Thurston decided to sit and reflect on his time with Martha.

The thoughts bounced between hatred of Martha, hatred of himself, and an uncertain acknowledgment that what she said was true. It burned into his soul the idea that he lacked conviction or purpose. That true conflict evaded him. Or rather, he evaded conflict.

And he wasn't even sure if that was what she meant at all. He poured himself another glass of soothing milk and paced the floor. There didn't seem to be a correct answer to what Martha expected. Could he have punched a wall when he saw Brandon shirtless in his living room? Of course, but why should he have? Martha was beautiful in her own small, black, gothic way. Much like a raven. Dark, shining, but often found digging through the trash.

But maybe Martha meant more than that. There was this twinging pain that welled from deep within him. He thought it was the pain from his shin irradiating upward into his stomach and eventually all the way to his eyes, but that couldn't have been it. He cried and wasn't sure why.

There wasn't much love for Martha. And the lack of excitement in their relationship weighed on Thurston. There hadn't been any novelty in quite a while. Yet, a stream of tears flowed steadily out of Thurston's eyes.

He thought about it for a second and pulled out the two numbers that he hoped could comfort him: Tony's pizza and his mother's. He considered the two options carefully. One would bring him immediate comfort and understand the plight of going through tumultuous relationships and be able to give steady-handed advice. The other would only lead to a bloated stomach and irritability. Thurston decided to go with the former and called Tony's.

After placing his order, he hoped that hearing from his mother would give him some relief from the circumstances, and despite all his prior knowledge of his mother, he dialed her phone number for comfort.

Rosemarie Ford gave birth to Thurston two weeks after her forty-second birthday. As a younger woman, she modeled and, as she aged, held onto her beauty. Her hair was bobbed and black, and her skin was taut, and each smile seemed somewhat painful against her wrinkleless skin. She was vain and beautiful and increasingly cold. For all of her beauty, she lacked any sense of maternal empathy. It was only out of abject desperation that Thurston dialed her number.

The phone rang as he sipped at his milk. He stopped crying. Martha's sudden departure numbed his emotions and all plans for the day, but it didn't numb his swollen, throbbing shin. A red and blue bruise was raised from the bone, and Thurston traced over it with his fingers.

Thurston flipped the blinds open and closed as he waited for his mother to answer. Martha's complaints echoed through his head with each flip. Flipped open. Throughout the course of their relationship, she badgered him until she got her way. He hadn't always been a pushover, he thought to himself. Flipped close. On their second date, Martha had drank too much, and Thurston reminded her that he still needed to study for a test the next day. At first, she whined, then insulted him, and finally laid down on the sidewalk and told him to leave her there because she was having fun. The taxi pulled up, and he explained that after studying, they could go back out, which was a blatant lie. She loaded herself into the back of the car and promptly fell asleep. Flipped open. But each time she wanted and took, he acquiesced a little more until she became a giant, and he grew so small that he barely recognized himself.

The phone continued to ring. Had he called Martha's bluff, perhaps she would have stayed, he thought to himself. He turned the call to speaker phone and worked to untag himself on anything that she had posted. The pictures of the two of them were quickly archived on his profile. A smile inched its way across his face as he realized that he could take it a step further. He went into each app and deactivated himself one by one. The less Martha was able to glean from the internet, the likelier she was to call him or try to see him. At least, that was what he hoped. During that build-up of anticipation, he'd have time to perfect his big, come-back-to-me speech for her.

The phone went to voicemail, and Thurston hung up. The manic smile faded from his face as he realized that social media wasn't the only way for people to find information. His eyes darted around the room as a new plan birthed. He rummaged through his book bag and notebooks. He needed each of his classes' syllabi, and he decided to notify his professors that he'd need an immediate two-week leave of absence. The lie could be that a family emergency across the world required his immediate attention, and he requested make-up work. Perhaps his parents developed mono and kept spreading it between themselves and their respective mistresses, and only he could untangle the mess of kissing disease.

Thurston's eager mind turned to pride, and he was certain that the grand gesture would show Martha that he could stand up for himself.

Pride fell away with a thud as the doorbell rang. Thurston also fell to the floor in fright and crept toward the door, reluctant to look through the peephole. He pushed himself to his feet and, with a swift and sudden force, pulled the door open.

"Jesus Christ," the pizza man yelped. Thurston yelped back at the sight of the pizza man and nearly toppled over backward. Both men stood in the doorway and clutched their chests.

At that moment, his heart pounded, and eyes bugged, his senses heightened in anticipation of inevitable doom. Thurston decided that he needed to go to his parents for his two, although he'd probably make it three, week furlough from reality. If Martha decided to stop by the apartment, it would only add to the air of intrigue. Thurston thanked the delivery driver and apologized for the fright. He then packed a bag for a long trip.

CHAPTER THREE

THE ROAD ALONG THE RIVER ROSE AND FELL WITH THE modest hills. Thurston drove over the speed limit and cut corners to keep the car steady. The middle line was a mere suggestion as the car glided back and forth between the lanes. He knew no one would be on the road this late at night, and the police didn't patrol the neighborhoods on this side of the river.

There was no reason for the hurried pace to Rosemarie Ford's house. The house was doubtless buttoned up for the evening, not a movement to be made for at least five more hours. Thurston's father worked early; a fact of which Thurston had been made keenly aware. He didn't doubt that his father worked early, and he even believed that his father did, in fact, do something, especially something that was worthwhile of money and apparently heaps of it. But as far as Thurston knew, his father worked in business, a vague, indeterminate idea of offices and high rises. The business, its subsidiaries, and its products were uncertain elements lost on Thurston, and for his sake, when people asked what his father did, he'd give a half-hearted reply and say, just business. It's far better to be vague than untruthful.

The house rose from its foundation in a grotesque and unsightly way. It was nearly six thousand square feet with a four-car garage. The Tuscan entryway sat between two large Southern plantation columns, a bay window adorned one half of the house, a circle window peered above the archway, and rectangle windows littered the other side of the house. A Japanese-style garden led to the pool house. The house, the garden, and the surrounding property were designed and maintained by his mother, the illustrious Rosemarie Ford.

Rosemarie had lofty visions for her son and the entirety of the Ford family; the estate was just a small piece of that grand vision. She bought retired greyhounds and gently euthanized them, swept into dying neighbors and purchased tax-liened houses to flip and sell to gentrifying white couples, and donated substantially to Baxter State College to ensure Thurston's admittance. Thurston admired his mother during his childhood. Her large jewelry and white teeth seemed a distinct contrast to his sunken eyes and blotchy skin. He often wondered how an elegant woman such as she could birth such a feckless creature. He wasn't the only one to wonder that. More often than not, teachers and parents exclaimed, "This is your mother?" mouths agape and eyes bugged. Thurston felt complimented at first until he realized that everyone was not overwhelmed by his mother's beauty but underwhelmed by his clear lack of it.

Although Thurston fell far short of her ideal for a son, Rosemarie reveled in the fact that he would never accomplish more than her. She could lament about the stress and how all-engrossing her life could be without ever worrying that his life would surpass hers in any way. She made sure that she reminded him of his smell or yellowed teeth. If that didn't work, she would badger him about school or girls, etc. Anything to keep her heel on his throat. All was fair game to make sure Thurston understood his place, which was somewhere below the greyhounds and above the koi.

It wasn't lost on the young man that he was intentionally entering the jackal's den. There was comfort to be found in the typical; he knew what to expect from both Rosemarie and his father. Rosemarie would harp about leaving school and all the work she had put into his admittance. If she'd had half the support that he does, she'd be President of the United States, that sort of thing. His father would be aloof, but not in a hilarious, inept way. When Thurston was younger, he was teased for his yellow teeth by someone other than Rosemarie; Thurston asked his father how to handle feeling bad. His father looked over from his email, peered down his long nose at Thurston, and said, "Don't do that."

At that time, he wasn't sure what it was exactly he wasn't supposed to do. Originally, he assumed his father meant don't spend too much time worrying about what other people think. Then, Thurston realized he probably meant don't interrupt his father's very important email time.

Home life was a different chaos than Martha but a chaos that could be anticipated, so Thurston quietly made his way into his room and laid down for the night.

After a restless night in his childhood bed, the door burst open to Thurston's dark, dank room. His father peered inside, said nothing, and slammed the door shut. Thurston jumped at the sudden sound. He rubbed his matted eyes. He ached and groaned as he made his way to the door. The idea of a sabbatical to clear his heartsick vanished. A strong smell of burned coffee beans filled the kitchen. Despite his father's stable and exceptional salary, the man refused to indulge in anything other than the cheapest and most basic home goods. Big house, a necessity, an expensive Jaguar for his wife, but, of course, and their lives absolutely depended on over-the-top, lavish vacations. But something other than burnt dirt for coffee, please don't be absurd.

Every decision needed calculation and consideration. A spreadsheet for household expenses that included a subsection titled "Leisure Activities" with a subcategory of "Fun" and a smaller category under that was titled "Family." The family budget included vacations, televisions, and gifts. Also included in the family budget was a yearly five-dollar expenditure for "Miscellaneous," which Thurston could only surmise was intended for a pack of gum and a Coke. Perhaps all these contrivances allowed his father to be the business savant he seemed to be. He obviously couldn't be bought, as earthly desires meant nothing; for God's sake, he only budgeted five dollars a year for a Coca-Cola and a pack of gum. Ignoring Thurston, one could assume that Mr. Ford was a middle-management, upper-middle-class eunuch. The idea of drugs and women as vices was laughable to Thurston's father. There seemed to be only one vice that he indulged in: charred grocery store chain coffee beans.

"I didn't know you were coming home." his father stated matter-of-factly. His phone lay face down in front of him. A banana carefully perched on the side of his plate outlined his granola and yogurt main course.

"Martha and I broke up," Thurston said. He paused for a moment to allow for a sympathetic reaction, but after a beat, he continued. "I wanted to get out of the apartment for a few days. Just to escape my feelings," he explained. His chair's legs banged against the table and screeched along the floor as he sat next to his father. Thurston mouthed, "Sorry," and pulled out his phone.

"I read a post on Onyx recently, and do you know what it

said? It's recommended that you meditate for at least ten minutes every morning before looking at your phone." Thurston's father said. He pulled the banana peel one side at a time to its end. The long, singular, peeled pieces laid two inches from his plate in a neat pile.

"You read on your phone that you should take a break from phones?" Thurston paused for a moment. "I didn't realize you were having a spiritual awakening." Thurston held his phone above his head and slowly set it face down. The banana peel pile yearned to be knocked over. Thurston tapped his fingers in anticipation.

"Not a spiritual awakening. Not that all." The eunuch never quite understood sarcasm. "It is supposed to help you focus through the workday. It is a productivity hack," his father explained.

"I will take that into consideration the next time I need to be productive."

Thurston left the table and wandered the estate. The house was decidedly gaudy; however, Thurston didn't hate it for its lack of cohesive architecture. He hated the feelings the house evoked. It was a quiet, isolating prison, thirty minutes from the nearest store and no sense of real stimulation. After his father left for work, Thurston went from room to room, peered inside, and rummaged. He considered playing video games or watching a movie, but he settled on productivity, inspired by his father's meditative insistence, and productivity became his mantra for the day. There aren't many times in life when one is able to push pause and make a concerted effort toward something, at least without the intervention of police or mental health facilities.

The morning crept along without the distractions of endless newsfeeds and alerts as his phone laid face down in the kitchen. He considered meditation but was unsure of how to go about doing it, and the urge to grab his laptop and look up the best meditation methods seemed counterproductive. He filled another cup of cheap, burnt coffee and stared out the window at the Japanese garden. Birds danced around the koi pond in the crisp morning air, and Thurston's mind wandered. He thought back to his lonely childhood and the summer afternoons laid out on the lawn filled with dreams of pirates and treasure hunting and going to Mars and scaling Everest. The dreams and life unfulfilled seemed so distant that Thurston felt destined to live a life of boring comfort. Disengaged from his dreams but endlessly entertained and warm.

Thurston watched the birds waddle toward the pond and enter slowly. One small step at a time and then a wiggle before being completely submerged and then popped back up at the surface. He considered his oldest childhood fantasy: a vague dream of him against an impossible natural force. He dreamed of storm chasing and crab fishing and mushing across the Arctic. A beard would adorn his wrinkled face, and with eyes squinted, he'd peer at the vast sea or an untamed mountain range. The typical idea of manhood, a Hemingwayesque mentality toward life, to fight and truly love. He rubbed his chin as he wondered what it would feel like to be bearded.

"You've come home." His mother's voice broke his daydream. The floor squeaked as she glided toward her son. As small and delicate as she was, her presence filled the room.

Thurston forced a smile toward her. He wished to be allowed to think until he found his purpose, and his mother certainly hadn't helped with that in the past. His shirt draped over his thin frame. It had only been one day since the Martha incident, and already he felt thinner. His collarbone jutted through his shirt.

"You don't have class today?" His mother asked. She pried. There was malice in her voice.

Thurston turned to her, completely shaken from his trance. His mug was cold, and the milk had pooled in the center of the coffee. "You know, I have been thinking about school and Martha and life, and I realized that I don't really know how to handle it all. Every time I'm able to juggle two of them, the third always seems to hit the floor."

Rosemarie nodded along. The teacup scratched as she placed it on the glass table. "Thurston, since you were a boy, I tried to instill in you how special and smart you were. I thought I was setting you up to succeed. I didn't want you to feel insecure or not confident, but I can see now what a mistake that had been. I shouldn't have lied to you back then. Life for you is *this*. Whatever it is that's going on now, it won't change, it will just get slower and lonelier for you."

Thurston stood. The birds in the koi pond seemed to enjoy the chaos inside as they stared back at the duo. He outstretched his hands and pulled one finger at a time until they popped. His mother's grimace turned to a scowl as she realized that he was deliberately annoying her, and each pop took longer than the last.

"You are right, mother. Thank you." Thurston said and heel-turned out of the room. The birds cheered behind him.

"You'll understand what I mean someday. Life and happiness aren't for everyone."

Thurston shivered. His headache returned and spread from between his eyes and back straight through his brain. The house echoed with emptiness. An empty house for an empty family. Thurston racked his memory to find a moment when his mother showed him warmth. Not love or moments of selflessness but unexpected warmth. The small favor that most even show toward strangers. The aspect of humanity that graced countless stories. Thurston wondered if she'd ever been warm to anyone.

Only one night and Thurston knew that he had overstayed his welcome. He collapsed on his bed. A twenty-four-hour disappearance was hardly noteworthy, and Martha hadn't even been given an opportunity to miss him yet, let alone worry. No, going back to school was off the table. He stood and paced around the bedroom. An Indiana Jones poster hung on the wall, and small ornate figurines from his dad's trips abroad lined the desk. The bookshelf contained volumes upon volumes of adventure stories. Westerns and expeditions and treasure hunters had filled his childhood. The yellow-tattered covers of National Geographic bookended his favorite series, The Lost Tribe of the Amazon.

He stared at the bookcase, and with a shot, he fell to the floor and rummaged underneath the bed. He pulled out item after item. A single sock, an old pair of headphones, an eighth-grade yearbook, until finally, he found what he had been searching for: a colored topographical map of the entire United States. His dad had bought it for work and used it to plot his sales district. There were pen marks and curse words sporadically across the map. "Fuck I-95" emblazed prominently on the East Coast. Even with the extra markings, the map was perfect. He imagined himself traipsing to San Francisco with only his backpack and the map.

The options seemed obvious. Head west or north, both ripe with adventure. Thurston's uncle lived in Maine, and he leaned toward heading north. Martha and his mother's words bounced in his head. "You don't stick up for yourself. You never do anything spontaneous," the memory repeated. He placed the large map firmly on the desk and grabbed a pen from the drawer. He closed his eyes and held the pen over the map. "Please don't be Ohio," he said as he lifted the pen high above his head. He closed his eyes and dropped it. The pen thudded and rolled away along the floor. Thurston inspected the map for new marks. He found a line through western Kansas, and his heart dropped, but as he followed it further west, there was a small smudge found on the other side of the border in Colorado, or at least that's what Thurston convinced himself. His face relaxed, and he breathed in and out with a decisive sigh. Colorado.

He looked over the state. Nothing east of Denver struck him as worth traipsing to, so he began to search for a town that called out to him. He read through names in the mountains: Salida, Crestone, Telluride, Aspen. None seemed to pull him in until he saw Idlewild.

The name coursed through his mind as he said it aloud. A place of relaxation and adventure, he thought. What a perfect place to hide from reality.

CHAPTER FOUR

Avery Salis needed to prove herself. No matter the weather, or rather in spite of it, she always walked to work. She figured that if she could accomplish a little bit of exercise first thing every day then she was ahead of most in this country.

But every morning different annoyances seemed to sprout from the city's sewers. For three mornings in a row, the city ruined her outfit. She tripped, crossing the street in front of the office building. Her knee skidded her to a stop and rubbed a big, tire-colored rip along the outer seam of her pants. The next day, a car splashed black street water across her yellow cotton sweater. The sludge water speckled islands of mud; she patted the speckles gently to keep them from smearing as she stood in disgust, waiting for the crosswalk sign. The third morning had been the most successful as she made it all the way to the coffee shop outside the office and then promptly spilled it down the front of herself as she struggled to open the door.

And every one of those mornings, men—the definition of sprouted sewer annoyances—called out to her.

"Oh, hey, baby. Where you going today?" She heard above

the sound of her headphones. She smiled at them and mouthed, "Hello." She understood how she looked, at least to those not paying attention to her stained and torn outfits. She was tidy and manicured, and had, on more than one occasion, been called cold and snobby.

Sometimes, these men would follow her for a beat. They walked closely behind her, and she could nearly feel their stale breath through their coffee and cigarette-stained teeth. She would move quietly and quickly and refused to say anything derogatory or belittling to these cretins.

Avery needed to prove to the world that she wasn't snobby. Her family was what most Americans would consider "old money," which only meant that her father's father had been lucky enough to own mineral rights in the twentieth century. Her father, too, reeked of wealth and breeding, and both tried to endow Avery with the same ideals. Her mother was a Korean immigrant and, for different reasons, wanted Avery to take after her conservative and even-keeled grandfather.

And as with any family, hers came with certain expectations. The wealth seeped into all aspects of those expectations and twisted them into a lack of any real choice for Avery. There were constant reminders that everything she worked hard on wasn't fully hers. Her grandfather paid for college. Her dad put the money down for her condo. Every time she needed to ask her mother for money, Avery was reminded how much she had sacrificed to make it to America. However, she seemingly always failed to mention that her immigrant journey would have gone much differently had she not ended up in the same computer science course that Peter Salis was taking and that her pregnancy followed shortly thereafter. But alas, her mother kept an air of victimhood just for such occasions.

Avery decided, to prevent her snobbish breeding from bearing itself, she would greet every cat caller and playboy that

spoke to her on the way to work. She understood that the gross
street harassers were beneath her, but she didn't have to let
them know that she knew that.

On this particular morning, Avery's outfit made it to the
office. There were no stains or rips, and she walked confi-
dently inside. She worked at Onyx, a new up-and-coming
smartphone application that specialized in authenticity, or
at least that was the claim. Little bits of bright authenticity
with the intention of being shared with the world in a deliberate and curated place. Avery understood and was okay
with the hypocrisy. And it helped that the job was fine.
Nothing about it was too demanding, and the pay seemed to
be enough to keep her family at arm's length. Her grandfather was even impressed at first, as Onyx also had a division
for oil and gas accounting services, but his smile faded as
she explained that she was working as an executive
assistant.

"So you're a secretary." He gruffed. His whiskers scratched
the microphone as he spoke.

"It's more than that. I run a lot of the timesheet reports and
host a lot of meetings. It's a lot like being a junior executive."
Avery explained. Her cat tugged at her leg, and she kicked him
away.

"Well, what do your parents think of all this?" He said and
took a sharp, sniffing breath.

"I think they're happy that I won't be asking for help with
groceries," Avery said. Avery's cat hopped onto the couch and
meowed directly in her face. She raised a finger to shush him.

"Sure." Her grandfather said. His tone came through
clearly. "I just don't understand why you had to go to college
across the country and now work so far away. If you move back
to Houston, I'll get you a better-paying job, and you won't be a
damn secretary."

She thanked him and explained that she wasn't a secretary as calmly as she could.

But most days, she felt like a damn secretary, especially on that morning as she carried a tray of specially ordered coffee into the conference room. A short, bald coworker with a title that far exceeded his abilities looked at Avery and didn't say a word. "Good morning," Avery said to the little man. "Is Magnus in today?"

"Shouldn't you have his schedule?" The little man gave a snort. "He's supposed to be in. But I think he's got a flight to catch this afternoon."

"Great," Avery said. She refused to look at the shiny-headed man as she left the room. There were two types of men that worked at Onyx: the handsome, decidedly privileged and the sniveling wieners who were also privileged but lacked the ability to realize it. This coworker was the latter. Their boss, Magnus, on the other hand, was a mixture of both.

Magnus Levine also needed to prove himself. Much like Avery, he was of wealthy stock but of the European variety. Born to a French couple that resided part-time in New York, he graduated from Wharton and moved to Cleveland to show his family that he could make it anywhere. Everywhere he went, people bestowed multiple chances on him, and he lucked into higher and higher roles. He worked hard, but his parents whispered in his ear that it was never enough; any accomplishment of his was due in large part to their generosity. There needed to be a constant push to prove himself.

Magnus created Onyx to help him make money to pursue bigger ambitions. There was never a point in his life where he felt passionate about social media, and it never seemed to be a worthy goal to pursue, and yet, here he was with a successful and thriving social media firm.

Avery wandered the office. Magnus wasn't at his desk, and

the lunchroom was empty, so she decided to look through his calendar to see if she'd forgotten an appointment. His calendar was always a mess, meetings piled upon meetings. There was never a free fifteen-minute window for Magnus. He even went so far as to schedule his exercise breaks and give himself time to reflect.

There was no forgotten appointment, and Avery wondered if she should worry. She left the coffee on his desk with a note, "No milk," and went into the break room. There was a ping-pong table and a row of microwaves. "Have any of you seen Magnus this morning?" She asked the group next to the coffee machine.

"I haven't seen him." A sniveling wiener replied.

Avery left the break room and thought she heard something from the closet. She pulled the door open slowly and looked inside to find Magnus. He stared up toward the ceiling. "What are you looking at?"

"Oh," Magnus said. The tone sounded frightened, but he didn't move. "I'm just thinking, actually. I come in here every morning to center myself before the day. I guess I just got a little lost in thought." His head shifted down from the ceiling, and his eyes locked with Avery's. His eyes were blue, and his blond hair was kept cropped against his large head. He was handsome, Avery couldn't deny it, but there seemed to be something off. Perhaps it was the way he kept his teeth clenched when he wasn't speaking. "While I have you here, can I ask you something?"

"I remembered to tell them no milk this time. I didn't want you to have another emergency in the middle of a meeting." Avery anticipated.

"Thanks, but I was going to ask, do you like me?" Magnus said, his eyes still locked with Avery's.

"Um," Avery said. Her face felt hot, and she stammered to

find the words. "I, uh, yeah. I like you as a boss. If that's what you mean."

Magnus stared back up toward the ceiling as he searched for words. "I think what I'm asking is, am I likable? A recent user survey landed on my desk this morning, and my likability is at an all-time low. We put out the survey because of that hit piece the Post put out. 'I was integral in the dismantling of the protests in Portland,' at least that's their claim." He paused for a moment and looked toward Avery to make sure she was still listening. He needed an audience. "But to tell you the truth, I don't have many friends here. And I think that's a better indication of me not being likable. Of course, those guys in Portland wouldn't like me; the media has smeared my name. I'm beginning to think that I should have moved to the Bay or New York like everyone else."

"Cleveland is tough. I ask myself that same question on a weekly basis. But I needed to get away from my family." Avery said. Her blush faded.

"I understand. No one in my family does. They still wish I moved home to help run their firm. 'That's why we sent you to college.' Anyway." His voice trailed off. Avery had never seen him so sensitive before. He looked like he was on the verge of tears.

"Well, I think you're great and probably able to make friends anywhere," Avery reassured him. She wanted to reach out and give him a pat on the shoulder but stopped herself. "I think I know something we can do. We'll do an internal pulse survey. It'll give everyone an opportunity to talk about how likable you are and the great work that you're doing around here."

"You think that's a good idea?" Magnus asked.

"I think it's a great idea." Avery lied.

CHAPTER FIVE

ALL ROADS LEAD TO A DESTINATION. SOME ROADS LEAD elsewhere and are everywhere, but Thurston walked along a two-lane road that seemingly led nowhere. Of course, there were nowheres in cities too. They littered back-alley side roads and spaces behind vacant lots. Suburbs were mostly filled with vapid, fast, convenient nowheres; towns full of row after row of safe, ordinary nowheres. But Thurston found himself in a rural nowhere somewhere near the state line with miles upon miles of nothingness in between.

Thurston shuffled his feet and kicked the same rock every three steps. The trees grew denser, and night darkened as he moved along the lonely stretch of highway. As night approached, his resolve waned. The idea to strike out seemed great in the morning, grew uncertain in the afternoon, and had become inconceivable with the cold of night.

His backpack concealed his father's large, annotated AAA atlas. He marked waypoints every ten miles, and he determined that at his current pace, it would take three months to make it to Colorado. The beauty of the map captured Thurston's wondrous nature. He laid it flat across a park bench and stared for hours. "We should head west. Of course, of course, but what of the creek and this endless expanse," he said to himself and cackled.

The map promised things unspoken. New women, new ideas, an unknowable challenge, and he loved it all. One thing Thurston had not accounted for while pouring over maps and daydreaming was the relative ease of using modern plumbing. The excitement of striking out had kept his bowels at bay, but he knew that wouldn't last. He also realized that there would be stretches of his journey where trees wouldn't be a certainty, which sent a frightful shiver down his back. A bathroom break with nothing but the cold wind against his bare bum hardly delighted Thurston.

These epiphanies led the whole plan to become askew. Perhaps spending every minute away from civilization was unnecessary. There would be no real risk of adventure until he had passed through Nebraska or Kansas.

Nobody would know if he cheated his way into the adventure. Jack London spent most of his life on a Hollywood ranch and only a few months in the tundra, and he was the quintessence of adventure. This gave Thurston an idea. He laid the map back down on the bench and decided for the sake of quickening the adventure aspect of this journey and really start getting into the muck and ruck of it all, he'd hitchhike to the nearest town and take a greyhound to Denver and continue his trek from there. He pointed himself toward the next town and prayed for a bus station.

The first town along his route was the small enclave of Saxton. And the town was particularly strange, especially at night. It was full of old, rusty industrial factories and chimney stacks, except the industry had moved to Asia and left only the skeleton of the depleted factories. Each block echoed the last with a single gas station and a tire shop, but only every third one remained in business. The town reeked of mildew and the sharp tang of rust. Empty factories stood like skeletal giants on the horizon, their broken windows staring vacantly at nothing. Not a single soul stirred—not a breath of wind, not even the sound of distant cars. It was like the town had been swallowed by a silence so deep it felt like a tomb. The inconsistency of the gas stations caused Thurston to skip the first one he had come upon and hoped that the next one would be a bit cleaner.

Sores opened along his big and small toes. Thurston failed to pack band-aids for the trip, and he cursed himself with each careful hobble. If he walked on the balls of his feet, the small toe took less damage, but it caused the big toe a lot more grief, and a water-filled blister lined the outside edge of that toe. He compromised and seesawed between the balls of his feet and the outside. The wobble and the backpack gave him the crazy, homeless advantage, and everyone gave him plenty of room as he walked down the road.

As he hobbled toward the gas station, he realized he had not been eating. His gaunt appearance was accentuated by deep, black circles around his eyes. His cheeks hollowed, and his mouth hung agape as he gasped for air, the only real sense of nutrition his body seemed able to obtain.

This had been his longest bout alone, and at first, he worried that he'd be bored spending so much time lost in thought. But hunger had surpassed boredom, and his mind seemed stuck on food. Bread didn't keep well in a backpack, neither did bananas, and he tossed both brown and mushed items out as soon as he could. Apples were okay, but he hadn't risked meat or vegetables. His steadfast options were nuts and jerky and trail mix. These, evidently, had not been supplying his brain with enough nutrition, and he found himself having conversations out loud but only with himself.

As he walked further and further down the road, hunger, or at least how he previously knew hunger, evolved. Hunger no longer seemed a means to end stomach cramps but more of a base desire that he had learned to live without. The pangs left. Jesus and Buddha fasted, and they were enlightened and spiritual. Thurston held that thought close as he made his way. All he had to do was get to the next gas station, and unlike Jesus, there were no devilish tormentors to be seen. He held his head higher as enlightenment filled the place his stomach used to live.

In a way, his thoughts became clearer. The fog of Martha and his mother and school all lifted as he propped himself against a tree. His mouth still hung open, and he gasped for food in the air, but still, his stomach felt empty. The answer to life's problems seemed to rumble out his gut and say, "Feed me."

Thurston laughed and said, "I'll feed you in a bit. Now, be quiet." He wondered if the simulation we lived in was powered by food. He licked his lips and craved salt. Potato chips with cheese, bagels with capers, and piles of enchiladas all danced in his head. Thurston had become Hunger, eater of anything.

He stood. His body propelled him toward the gas station. His fear of sanitation vanished as food beckoned him onward. The EZ Fill Up lit the dark road as a beacon of hope, and Thurston glided toward it with ease. Maslow's hierarchy quaked as he entered the store. He had it all: warmth, food, and shelter, and he planned on taking full advantage of each. He marched toward the bathroom and turned the hot water on. It was the first time that he had looked in the mirror in two days, and he jumped at the sight of himself. "Oh," he said and splashed his face with water. It never occurred to him how quickly life outside caused people to look homeless. His face and hair were matted with mud; he picked out the hardened bits from his hair and threw them in the sink.

In disgust with himself, Thurston left the gas station without buying any food. The man behind the counter knew him only as a homeless bum who washed up in the bathroom, and that hurt Thurston's fragile pride. He wiped a tear from his face and headed toward the woods across the highway.

In the middle of the night, rain pelted him on the forehead. Thurston opened his eyes, and water splashed from his forehead directly into them. He blinked and swatted away the rain, then tossed and rolled inside his hammock, but the water targeted his ear and the side of his cheek. No amount of thrashing seemed to keep him out of the drenching wet. He sighed and crawled out of the sleeping bag and fell to the ground. He rolled up his bed and left the hammock. The overpass was less than a mile away, and he walked to it in the rain, hoping that no other vagrants had already sought shelter there.

After three days on the road, the pressure of being a person flitted away. Thurston watched from the overpass as a raven picked at roadside trash for twenty minutes and realized that he had more in common with that bird than Martha, or really anyone else for that matter. Martha had not come by the apartment, and Thurston knew that. He knew that this grand gesture of adventure and passion would be lost on her. He rolled his sleeping bag up, attached it to his rucksack, and headed back toward the gas station.

A sedan crept alongside Thurston, and a small boy pressed his head to the glass. Thurston smiled and waved at the weird little boy, and the car sped away. Thurston sighed. A homeless man watched Thurston approach the store. His dog sat beside him and yapped as the voluntary vagrant drew closer. The man took a cup of change and shook it at Thurston. Thurston looked at him, pointed to himself, and muttered, "Homeless."

The word fell out of his mouth without a thought. It hit the ground, dusted itself off, and tried to crawl back into Thurston's mouth and mind. An unwarranted word for what Thurston was doing. Thurston's eyes filled with tears.

The beggar smiled and tried to comfort the tearful young man. "It'll be alright. We are all here."

Thurston nodded along. Homeless: a word tied to addiction and hardship. A word that created illusions of tough existence and tragedy. But Thurston knew that homeless wasn't the word to describe himself. Perhaps, over-privileged and unfulfilled, but homeless was not the right word. A young man on a budget backpacking trip across America lacked the guttural sympathy for which he longed.

The door swung open, and a bell rang. A ragged woman with a short, gray bob looked up from the counter and yelled to Thurston that backpacks weren't allowed in the store. He agreed and placed it outside next to the beggar and dog. "Will you watch this," he said and went back inside.

The aisles were lined with processed donuts and bagged boiled eggs. A jar of pickles, one dollar each, sat on the counter in front of rows and rows of Marlboro and Newports. A sign stated that ZigZags were to only be sold with a bag of tobacco and not by themselves.

Thurston found a beautiful stash of clearance items, all of which were slightly expired and processed. He gathered a box of Slim Jims and bags of potato chips and waddled toward the counter. The gray-haired woman sighed as he raised a finger in patience. Thurston plopped sticks of cheddar and string cheese on top of the pile.

The cashier's thin, transparent fingertips moved quickly as she placed each item in the same plastic bag. The bag weighed down in the center and stretched the clear plastic so the world could view Thurston's insatiable appetite for artery-clogging meat sticks.

Thurston went outside and grabbed his wallet from the

backpack. He gave a thumbs up to the homeless man for watching the bag and paid for his feast.

The road wandered into fields of alfalfa. The hills were green and wet. Snails the size of half dollars slimed up toward the log Thurston perched himself on. He placed his dinner along the log. The chips crunched and melted in his mouth. He counted the individual grains of salt with this tongue.

The cheddar cheese stick had a grease layer, and Thurston patted it on his sleeve before eating it. The cheese tasted like plastic, so he tore a piece off and put it on the chip. The flavor of the plastic cheese elevated the salt in the chip, and his eyes rolled back in ecstasy. He broke off a piece of Slim Jim, stacked it with the cheese and chip, and plopped it in his mouth. The potato chip sandwich filled a spot that Thurston was unaware he had.

Each chip sandwich tasted better than the last, and before he was able to realize it, all of the chips had been eaten. Most of the Slim Jim remained, and he broke it into bite-size pieces and swallowed all of them in one bite. He leaned against the log and smiled. The snails crept closer, and ants congregated to pick up pieces of leftover chips and cheese.

Thurston prepared himself for the night. He rolled his sleeping bag out alongside the log and stretched his back. The day had been a success. The food replenished his mind and fortitude, and heading on his grand adventure seemed an attainable goal, even if it was still distant and lofty. He fluffed his backpack and laid down for the night. He found himself quickly asleep.

Terror struck three minutes past midnight. Thurston grappled with his sleeping bag and rummaged through his pack. All of his belongings lay on the ground, torn out from the backpack in a frantic haze, until he finally reached his headlamp at the bottom of the bag. He tossed the backpack away in frustration as he scrambled toward the nearest tree and grasped at his belt and pants button. A terrible moment occurred, and Thurston dared not look behind himself. With pants around his ankles, he waddled forward back to the camp, one large, careful waddle at a time. He grabbed toilet paper from the backpack and waddled backward at an even slower pace. Every movement was slow and deliberate as he felt his way back to the toilet tree.

The world spun around him. "This is how people die," he said aloud, "shitting themselves to death in the woods." The worst had already passed, and the guttural pain that had awoken him had stopped so he could reevaluate the situation. The gas station menagerie poisoned him. And his body convulsed in sickness. A newfound vigor overcame Thurston as he vowed to never not plan for pooping again. He cleaned himself and crawled carefully back to his camp.

It took every ounce of strength but sleep eventually overcame the young man. Thurston slept for an additional eight hours, wracked with spasms and shakes as his body digested the incredible amount of sodium. He existed past the point of being able to walk. Thus far he had averaged twenty-five miles a day, far short of his ambitious and unrealistic goal of three hundred and fifty miles per week. Even if he doubled every day for the next three days, he would still fail. Dew chilled him as he wrestled out of his sleeping bag, buttoned his trousers, and hurried away from the spot of the incident.

CHAPTER SIX

THE SENTIMENTALITY OF CHRISTMAS ALWAYS BRIGHTENED Thurston's mood. The lights and the feel-good music and the sweet treats lifted him up from even the most dire of circumstances. Oftentimes, his mother would put aside all of her condescension and petty jabs for a three-day span, the day before, during, and after Christmas, and for that small window, the Ford household had an air of normalcy. Thurston pulled out a grape-flavored Swisher Sweet and lit it as he leaned against a tree somewhere on the Missouri-Illinois border. New locations lost their luster hundreds of miles before as he entered into another Nowheresville along a dusty, two-lane highway cutting through cornfields.

The December air bit at him with every draw from the cigar. It filled his mouth with the grape flavor and burned his eyes as he tried to blow the smoke away from himself. While he was dating Martha, he smoked yellow American Spirits. He'd lean himself outside the bar next to the door while she ordered her fourth round. She would always order one round too many and expect him to hang out while she talked to the bartender about which Teenage Mutant Ninja Turtle would be into her music. Thurston didn't really understand the music or the heady Maoist references in the lyrics, but the cigarettes created the facade that he was really rather clever. They helped him fit in and created a sense of belonging.

He missed that feeling of belonging. He took another drag of the grape-flavored cigarillo and realized that no one could see him and that this facade was for no one but himself. It felt nice to do something for himself. It had been two hundred miles since he threw his cell phone in the river. There was no way of knowing what day or even month it was. He was certain that this cheap gas station cigar was his way of celebrating Christmas.

A hundred visions of what his family and friends must be doing filled his head. Of course, his mother would be pleasant. His cousin Eric would lament law school, and his sister Christina would explain why the justice system was another example of the bourgeoisie protecting its place in society by holding everyone else down. Thurston's father would be agreeable but not overtly because he would hate to accidentally encourage Christina's worldview. Uncle Bryan would have smoked a cigar himself, but not a cheap gas station one, something that he had imported. And they'd all be gathered around the table as Rosemarie carefully dished the plates.

Thurston closed his eyes; he smelled the pies coming fresh out of the oven and the sound of the ham being thinly sliced. He smacked his lips and took another drag of the cigarillo. The grape flavor wasn't distinct from the tobacco, and if he thought too much about it, he wanted to gag. It seemed to be a common occurrence and not particularly about the cigar itself. He'd get stuck in a thought and nearly paralyzed. This paralysis almost always upset his stomach, and he'd gag or wretch. Thurston found that life was best if he could suppress his thoughts. It also helped to have something mindless to fixate on, so he continued smoking. The highway that he lay beside was also the main street into a town. He thought the last sign said Cairo, but then he remembered Paducah, and both seemed like terrible places to be spending Christmas.

Although it was cold, there was no snow or wind. The cold crept up from the ground and the wet marshland. It hung to his clothes and made the cigar smoke hang suspended. The cold brought a stiffness to his heart. Perhaps it was nothing more than the holiday blues and missing the only pleasant time to be around family, but Thurston felt off. He wanted a celebration and to feel the Christmas Spirit, and by God, he was going to do it.

He rolled out his sleeping bag. The cold and despair weren't going to squander his holiday, so he hung socks from the tree beside him and piled a few rocks underneath as mock presents. The roadside camp silence mocked his dedication to holiday cheer, so in steadfast defiance, he began to whistle Good King Wenceslas as well as he could and thanked everyone for joining him as he placed a Clif Bar and a can of Spam out on the sleeping bag. "This will be a fantastic holiday season; I can just tell." And the rest of the group nodded along silently as he popped open the can of Spam and tore the wrapper for the granola bar.

He held the lit grape cigar between his forefinger and thumb and gave it a little spin. Unsure if a tobacco candle would be appropriate to ring in the birth of Christ, Thurston placed it in the gelatinous center of the spare pork cube and whistled even louder. The holiday cheer was infectious. He grabbed a present from underneath a tree and said, "Here you go, Jesus, happy birthday," then placed the rock neatly next to the makeshift birthday cake. "This is definitely a meal fit for the King of Kings."

Thurston was not exceedingly religious. There were rumblings of spirituality, especially when he felt scared or alone. The sheer frightfulness of existence was eased by the idea of a higher power. But the Ford family really only celebrated Christmas. They did adhere to the spirit and all of that; for them, it wasn't just a gross demonstration of capitalism and the consumption of toys and Frosty the Snowman movies. Besides a smorgasbord of food, the Ford household decorated the house in Middle American fashion: an outdoor nativity scene and white twinkle lights and a tasteful sign that read 'Bless this House.' It was a stark difference to the tacky architectural accouterments of the house. Even Rosemarie had enough of a sense of humor to dress her Buddha statue up as a chubby, Asian Santa Claus.

The desire to be home and the nostalgia of Christmases past conflicted Thurston. There would be no one to watch Miracle on 34th Street with or split a class of eggnog. It was the first time in the last two months that Thurston really considered giving up. No one would know or care if he gave up. In fact, if anyone is worried about him, they'd be relieved if he came back home. No explanation needed; he could just blame it on some sort of terrible amnesiac episode caused by an irritation in his digestion. The Spam certainly didn't help the matter and was another stark contrast to remind him of a real, well-cooked Christmas ham. The Swisher Sweet candle did not resemble twinkly lights, and it hardly made him think of Jesus. The grape flavor wafted up to his nostrils and made him wince. The smell while being smoked felt full and tasted good, but when not being smoked, it smelled stale and hurt Thurston's head.

He needed to get on the move. The closest town was due east, and although backtracking should have chapped his ass, he felt good about finding a neat place to celebrate the most wonderful time of the year. He was sure the good people of Carthage, Illinois, or was it Shelbina, Missouri, would welcome a wandering young man blown in on Christmas Day. Thurston took one final drag of the Swisher Sweet and then flicked into the ditch. He wrapped the Spam carefully in a t-shirt, placed it on the top of his backpack for later, and kicked the rock presents all around; they were terrible gifts anyway. Off he went, unsure of exactly where he would end up but with an overwhelming belief in the goodness of people and the power of the Christmas spirit.

The Missouri town, or perhaps Illinois or Iowa, seemed indistinguishable from the last dozen towns Thurston had traipsed through so far. It was especially odd that not one iota of Christmas spirit or festiveness existed, at least along the facades of the rundown downtown. There was a small gift shop with some old Halloween displays in the front window. The woman inside dusted a row of mason jars filled with assorted hard candy as Thurston walked inside. He smiled and gave a half wave to get her attention.

He cleared his throat, but the old lady's focus remained steadfast. He got a little closer, knocked on the counter, and cleared his throat at the same time. "Excuse me," he said. His knuckles rapped on the counter even harder, and he knocked the jar of sour fruit balls to the floor. Glass and balls were scattered throughout the store, and Thurston quickly tried to grab as many candies as he could.

"What are you doing?" She adjusted her glasses and then threw her hands up in the air in disbelief.

"Here you go," Thurston said. He held out his hand, full of candy balls and, without thinking, dropped them on the counter, and they rolled all over the place again.

"Just stop. Are you trying to ruin my day?" The woman said. Her hands were seemingly stuck in the air as she tried to understand why this weird bum came in to knock her candy display around.

"No, no, of course not. I came in to ask if any churches or community centers were doing anything for Christmas today. I'm a little homesick and was hoping for a pick me up." Thurston explained. He brushed the broken glass into a pile with his foot. The old lady looked on with her face twisted up in disgust.

"It's October 23rd."

Thurston stood for a second, confused and concerned, and his momentary paralysis did little to make him seem less like a creep. The faint threat of police filled the store, but Thurston couldn't quite make it out. "October 23rd," he said to himself. His arms hung limp and swung out from his body as he turned around. He knocked another two jars of candy to the ground with his confused and floppy arms. But he didn't care. He would have knocked down every jar in the store, if it would have helped him make sense of the date.

The threats and yelling continued, but none of that mattered. Perhaps he was having a stroke, he thought to himself. It would explain the broken jars and the limp arms and not being able to understand English. The mixture of Spam and Swisher Sweet could have caused a weird chemical reaction within him that allowed time to stop working. Although unlikely, perhaps he created a new illicit drug from his Jesus Christ Birthday Celebration.

If he had only been gone for five weeks, it was the longest, most miserable five weeks of his life, and Thurston wasn't sure if he could continue. At best, it was a fruitless endeavor, and at worst, he could get brain cancer from mixing nitrates and tar together in the name of Jesus.

He found a barrel in the alleyway behind the old lady's gift shop and propped himself up on it. He pulled out the can of

Spam from his backpack and ate it with his fingers. The meat, although now cold, still had the stale, bingo hall smell on it from being warmed by the cigarillo. Each bite tasted worse than the last, but he continued to eat it. He wasn't better than this food. He had created this situation, every aspect of it. He could be eating pizza and listening to Martha's incessant whining, but he chose to strike out. He chose to find adventure in this life and go west. He wasn't going to allow an old lady to bully him into giving up, even if she lied to him about the date.

His resolve returned, and he headed back west on the highway, away from town and toward what he hoped would be his future. He vowed to never ask anyone for the date again.

CHAPTER SEVEN

"I have always loved hearing your stories." The old woman said. She clapped her hands softly and slowly. Her every movement was deliberate as she reached out and squeezed the arm of the young lady she spoke to. The older woman smiled a goodbye and returned to her booth. Anna, the old woman, smiled at everyone she encountered and hoped for the best for the world.

Dottie, her lifelong best friend, sat in a lawn chair with her arms crossed. "See anything you like?"

"Of course. There are just so many talented women in our congregation." Anna said. The sign on their booth was lopsided, and Anna took a moment to fix it. "All set." She patted herself on the back and returned to her seat next to Dottie. The fair seemed quiet compared to previous years, and it worried Anna. "Did anyone come while I was gone?"

"Not to my knowledge," Dottie said and uncrossed her arms. The tension in her face had left as Anna sat beside her. And she sighed a deep life-giving breath. But the unease promptly returned when a couple carrying a baby approached their booth. Dottie struggled with happiness and found it short-lived and fleeting. In the last twenty years, Dottie had only been identifiably happy for a one-week period: from the moment she found out her husband perished in a car crash up to the day of his funeral. Relief washed over her as she realized that she no longer had to search for him from bar to bar. However, since then, she had settled into a routine of quiet discontent.

The pair of women's lives mirrored each other. Both grew up in Gail, Indiana, born into the life of poor Midwesterners. Their families brought the girls to the same Lutheran service every Sunday, and they went to the same schools. By their sixteenth birthdays, Dottie and Anna spent every weekend at the lake teasing boys and going bowling. That was until Dottie became pregnant the following spring.

The pregnancy caused a schism between the friends, and their lives drifted further apart when Anna left for college. Dottie felt stuck and was forced to marry her son's father; her disdain for him grew as quickly as his love for the bottle did. He could never be found at home, but a quick trip to each of the three bars in town would always reveal his location.

Anna met the man she married when he gave a lecture at the University of Indiana. He was an older television executive from Toronto and wanted to pamper Anna. She was the much younger second wife, and there were no expectations of children. She was free to pursue leisure activities, and that she did. She spent every afternoon at the tennis courts or at the pool. Unfortunately, both of their husbands died the same year, Anna's of old age and Dottie's of the aforementioned drinking.

Her first year as a widow aged Anna. All the conveniences of having someone to cater to her left a large hole in her life. Up to that point, she had never been alone, and the loneliness consumed her thoughts. She missed small and constant interactions and would seek conversation where she could. One day after her husband's death, while picking through the produce section, she saw Dottie across a stack of zucchini. "Dottie Miller?" Anna asked. The woman she saw seemed much older than Dottie and a lot meaner.

"Anna?" Dottie was genuinely surprised. She stood still as Anna pranced around the vegetable pyramid and hugged her. "What are you doing here?"

"Looking for a new husband." Anna laughed, picked up a zucchini, and waved it around in the air. Dottie stared at her. "I'm sorry," Anna said and placed the zucchini back on the display. "I lost Ed a few months ago and I'm still figuring it out."

"I heard. Frank is gone, too. But no use crying over spilled milk." Dottie said. She pushed her cart away from Anna, slowly at first. There was not one thing that she could think of that the two could talk about.

Anna followed.

"It's so funny I ran into you. I have been back in town for a while now, and I see the funniest people. You remember long arm Steven? He's still working at the bowling alley. I thought he was old when we were in school, but he's actually much older now. No idea why he keeps working. And I saw Brenda, still as sweet as ever. Do you see many people from school?" Anna asked. She leaned over her shopping cart toward her old friend.

"I try not to," Dottie said and pushed her cart a little faster. The wheel squeaked, and the cart jumped.

"You're too funny. You were always my funniest friend. When I lived in Toronto, I used to tell people all about that time in the cabin when you came out dressed in that robe and did the Richard Nixon impression. Oh, Lord. What great times." Anna smacked the cart and stopped in the aisle to laugh at the memory. Dottie seized the moment to try and get away.

"Well, it's been nice..." Dottie began.

"It has. Let's get lunch." Anna said. Following that reconnection and a few awkward lunches, the pair became roommates and decided to continue that way. They spent nearly every day together, from church bake sales to doctor's appointments to their quiet, nightly routine.

The couple with the baby browsed and Anna made coochie noises at the infant. "He's just so precious," she said.

"This is our first time in public, isn't it?" The young mother bounced the baby and said inches from its squished face.

Across the booth, Dottie said. "No, nothing on the table is gluten-free." The young father stared at her with a blank expression. Dottie's eyes tightened as she straightened the loaf of banana nut bread that the man had sat back down.

"That's too bad. We're on a strict gluten-free diet. It reduces sperm count and causes all sorts of inflammation." The man said.

"You're worried about sperm count?" Anna asked. She motioned to the small child that she presumed was his. "Oh, I'm sorry. I assumed you were a couple. This must be your niece." She tickled the tike's chin.

"Yes, you were correct to assume." He said. He reached out to his wife. "This is my child." He said aloud as if to reassure himself and the rest of the world. The woman hid the baby back under the swaddle blanket.

"Thanks for stopping by," Anna said. She waved at the couple. "What a beautiful young couple. Don't you think so?" She looked toward Dottie, who relaxed back into the chair with her arms crossed again.

"Gluten-free. When we were their age, nobody even thought about gluten, and guess what? There were still babies." Dottie sighed. "How long do we have to be here?"

"Only four more hours," Anna said and smiled at another group as they came close to the booth.

"Great," Dottie said.

"Oh, there's Pastor Doug!" Anna said and waved.

Pastor Doug was the brand-new pastor at All Paths Lutheran Church in Gail, Indiana. He started his tenure at All Paths after Pastor Stan Lindauer retired and at first received mixed reception. On the one hand, his being an outsider and newcomer, weeded the congregation quickly, all of whom claimed they didn't mind a fresh perspective but were quick to point out other reasons why they left the church that they had attended for so many years. "It's just hard to understand him," some would say. "I don't agree with his focus on the New Testament," others piped in. But Dottie and Anna were excited for the change.

"It's about time we had a young, handsome pastor," Anna said the day he was introduced as Stan's replacement.

"As long as he does Communion every week, I don't care," Dottie responded.

Pastor Doug approached the booth.

"How are you ladies doing today? Have you sold a lot of muffins?" Pastor Doug asked. He picked up the loaf of banana nut bread and placed it back down askew.

"We are fine," Dottie said. She picked the banana nut bread up for the second time and lined it back up in the formation.

"We are just wonderful. This is a great turnout this year. I think we'll definitely hit our donation goals." Anna said. Their table was still completely full of merchandise.

"I believe we will." Pastor Doug said. "Speaking of which, I have been brainstorming on how we can do the women's retreat a little differently this year."

Anna and Dottie exchanged glances. The yearly women's retreat had been in planning for four months, and the deposit was already set; every year, the group, led by Anna, spent three days at the Gail Country Club and split their time between tennis, worship, poolside gossip, and dinner.

"The deposit has been paid, Pastor Doug. The women here all really look forward to the weekend." Anna said. Dottie's arms returned to their crossed position.

"I have already spoken to the Country Club on your behalf, and they've agreed to return the deposit," Pastor Doug said smugly. He wore a button-up plaid shirt that hugged his belly. His arm fat rolled out from under the short sleeves. "You'll be really happy about the place we've chosen instead.".

"Well, aren't you going to tell us? There's no reason to be coy." Dottie urged.

"I'd like us to go to Idlewild, Colorado." Pastor Doug said.

"Colorado?" Anna said. "The Country Club really gives us a discount. There's no way today's craft fair will pay for Colorado."

"How will we even get there? I don't take airplanes, and I will not use the bathroom on a Greyhound." Dottie said.

"With God's grace, anything is possible." Pastor Doug assured them. "Also, my cousin works at a lodge there and should be able to get us a discount. I've visited a few times to cut loose and relax. I think you and the other ladies will really enjoy it. Peace be with you." He bowed at the pair and left.

"And also with you." Dottie and Anna responded in unison. They both racked their brains as they tried to think of how elderly women could raise money.

CHAPTER EIGHT

Magnus paused and raised his finger. The news of his likability survey came back, and he fell into the depths of wholesale self-improvement. He listened to motivational speakers and read mindset recalibration books; both helped Magnus realize that an air of mystique would only benefit his brand. His look and ability to discuss technology would only get him so far and obviously hadn't made him particularly likable. He dreamed of auditoriums filled with adoring geeks and beautiful journalists, all of whom would clamor for a few moments to speak with him. It wasn't enough for him to be rich and famous; he wanted unwarranted veneration. The type of power only a few ever gain.

But the finger raised something else inside him. It inspired confidence in his thoughts and allowed him to jump to assumptions about what others must think of him.

The first assumption he jumped to was that he was as dull as his company. The pause and finger raise felt lackluster. Perhaps because it wasn't in front of an audience, except for Avery. She watched him practice his walk and mannerisms in the mirror. The facade of his genius dropped as soon as she began to help with his likability endeavor.

The finger came down. "There needs to be more allure." The finger came back up and came down with a heavy sigh. "George Harrison went to India," Magnus said.

Avery stared at him. She watched the finger raise back up for a third time.

"Don't you have anything to say?" Magnus asked. He pranced toward her on the balls of his feet. "I need your expert and professional opinion." His finger held out before him as if covered in something that he didn't want to touch.

"The Beatles went to India. I think what I'm failing to grasp is the relevance to our situation. You aren't a rock star, Magnus." Avery said. The raised finger inched closer to her face.

Magnus dropped the finger and placed his hands on his hips. The office was empty except for the two of them. "I'm not a Beatle. I could be George, though. Quiet, handsome, Hindu." Magnus pulled at a thread on his shirt. "Steve Jobs tapped into it. As did Rudy Giuliani. Smart, spiritual leaders that everyone adores. And it will get more people to try Onyx."

Avery rifled through her backpack and pulled out a large notebook with the words "Make Magnus Likable" scribbled across the top. "I don't think tapping into the spiritual zeitgeist is going to make you any more approachable."

Magnus turned to her. His eyes beamed, and the finger rose again. "And what do you know about approachability?" Magnus grabbed Avery by the shoulders and squeezed. "Consider the irony: a spoiled rich girl teaches a self-made millionaire how to make the common folk like him. Do you get a good view of the plight of the working class from that ivory tower?" His eyes widened and real, unrehearsed excitement seeped from him.

Avery set her pen down and rolled her eyes. Her grandfather developed hearing loss around the time Avery began teething. She would exaggerate movements and reactions for his benefit, and exaggerated expressions were very helpful when dealing with Magnus. "Fine, I'll go. You obviously have this handled. Remind me again: how beloved and likable Steve Jobs was? Oh wait, I just remembered. Everyone thought he was an asshole."

Magnus slumped into his chair and wailed. His fists beat against the table, and he slapped himself across the head. "My ideas are derivative, and nothing good ever comes out of this stupid, stupid head." He timed the 'stupids' with the head slaps. He wept openly and aggressively.

Avery's eyes rolled again. She placed his juice tumbler in front of him. It contained carrot and celery juice with a heavy dose of jalapeno for a kick to keep him alert. Magnus wiped tears from his face and took a large swallow of the colon-cleansing brew.

"Thank you for always being so kind to me." Magnus gasped and reached toward Avery. "I want to be loved, but I am worried that the public will only see me as a fraud. Why did I sell that data to the police? Why must I cheat for success?" He whimpered but didn't have the strength for a proper wail. The train of thoughts rushed back as the jalapeno juice seared his tongue.

"I think that spirituality may be the key. Steve Jobs isn't a good example, but everyone does love the Beatles." Magnus began. He waited to see Avery's reaction. There were no eye rolls or sighs, so he went on.

"I think we should do a sabbatical, an American road trip. We can stop by Buddhist houses and little Christian huts and Scientology churches and the biggest ball of twine in Minnesota. Anybody that will speak to me, we will speak to. And that will only help us build my confidence, which will only make me more likable. We can host open forums where real people can tell me what they think about the app and about me. It'll be like we're modern hippies; except we'll be staying in hotels and spas most of the time." Magnus gulped down the celery juice, and his face grew red from fear and jalapeno sweat. Drops of bathroom urgency pooled at his brow, but he didn't dare move.

"Okay, that could work. When do you want to go on this life-changing quest?" Avery asked.

"As soon as possible." He breathed deeply to suppress the churning stomach juices. "A plan is counterintuitive to road inspiration. We'll leave tonight."

Surprisingly, Avery agreed. The suddenness of the plan inspired her. She stood and placed her work in her backpack. "Wait, wait, I didn't mean right now." Magnus swallowed another breath to counter his bathroom worry. "We can leave after we pack properly."

"Magnus, I'm sorry, but I disagree. We need to move now. This is the first idea you've had that is truly great, and there's no time to waste." She motioned for him to stand and swung her backpack over her shoulder. She held the door open and urged him outside.

The man prayed as he made his way toward Avery's Jeep. "I do not have a good feeling about setting off tonight. We haven't checked the weather or know which roads to avoid. I think it's best to lay down and take a Xanax, and we can leave first thing in the morning."

CHAPTER NINE

As Thurston hurried, he felt a familiar pain and gasped. The muscles in his legs tensed, and a spasm ran down his spine. He leaned forward and took ten deliberate and slow breaths; each exhale, he promised God devotion and newfound faith. It had been foolish of him to eat when he had been doing so well without food.

Thurston came upon a set of train tracks and decided to walk along them. He balanced himself on the rails for a few moments and then jumped from one tie to another, with sure-footedness to not step on the ground. This brief reprieve from thinking about his stomach helped, but he secretly hoped the tracks would lead him directly to a toilet. The shining beauty of a porcelain seat compared to a toilet tree had grown into a luxury. If there was no toilet, there was the perpetual hope that a train would hit him and put him out of his misery.

After four miles, Thurston found the next small town that dotted the map. The state highway became the main street and then small, abandoned banks and hotels lined both sides. The first floor's windows were smashed, and cats crawled in and out as they wandered along the empty roadway. Gray overcast blanketed the entire town in malaise. A wheelchair abandoned next to a defunct car wash struck Thurston as a profound statement of the matter of the things in this rural nowheresville. Although, it was the same as the last town and the town before that. Industry came and left, drugs filled the void, anybody with potential got out, and the rest were stuck in hopeless desperation. Thurston limped through the decay and clenched.

A mural decorated the side of the closest building. The mural was of a woman; in one hand, she held a glass of milk, and in the other, she held the corner to a banner that read "We support Dairy Farmers of America." The building sat next to a large park named Lammot Dairy Park. Toward the center of the park a plaque next to a bovine statue read "This park is dedicated to Bill and Jeanine Lammot. Proud supporters of Delmar County Farmers Market and the Hucker Children's Chorale."

A tear formed in Thurston's eye as he read the sign. He had hoped that it pointed toward a bathroom or, at the very least, explained how to get to one. It wouldn't have taken much to cheer the poor boy up. After a few moments of hopeless wandering, he eyed two portable toilets on the other side of the park and Thurston rushed ahead. His palms sweated. One of the restrooms was locked, and he slowly opened the door to the second. Flies exited in mass and flew into his eyes and mouth. He waved at them and peered inside the dark, portable water closet. He sat his backpack on the ground next to the portajohn. Green mold grew across the floor, and Thurston winced as he stepped inside. There had never been a moment that had pushed Thurston to the brink. Despair, anger, and acceptance all rushed forth as he relieved himself. The knowledge that a flashlight or a well-timed car wouldn't reveal the magnitude of his sickness relieved his soul.

Thurston sat in the small green plastic building for three full minutes. At two minutes, he breathed deeply and deliberately. The last minute, he thanked every deity imaginable and some of his own creation. He thanked the creators of plastic, the inventors of petroleum drilling, every person in the forestry industry, and the dozens of trees felled for toilet paper everywhere.

As he left the throne, it took only a moment to notice that his backpack no longer sat next to it. He looked behind the green portable building. He walked around the perimeter of the park.

A backpack snatched, stolen by thieves in the bright daylight next to a portable toilet in a dairy park. Thurston rubbed his head and squatted next to where the backpack had been. Warm dry socks, a copy of the New Testament and sage for good luck, his wallet, toothbrush, two condoms for unlikely scenarios, chapstick, and the map, all gone with the bag. Thurston reached into his empty coat pockets and wished that he had pinned a twenty somewhere.

Everything had been packed into its perfect compact place, and that place disappeared. He sat on a park bench and picked up a fallen branch. He snapped it between his fingers and picked up another. Snapped again and again until there was nothing left to gather. A pigeon walked up to the bench and looked toward the tree branch-breaking man. Thurston shook his head at the bird. "What would you do?" Thurston asked.

The pigeon shrugged and pattered away. Across the street, a reflection stared at Thurston. Gaunt with an angular jaw, sunken, sullen eyes, caverns into a soul that was drifting further and further into troubles. Unreality filled every crook and creak of the being before him, and Thurston jumped to his feet. The abyss stared back at him, and he felt frightened and invigorated.

Thurston bounded down the street. Every other storefront

was vandalized, and broken glass sprinkled the roadway, but his mania could not be contained. A backpack tethered him to the real world and Thurston watched as that real world vanished, wholesale. The entire trip was delusional. Joy found in comfort was delusional. Security found in numbers on a screen was delusional. As long as he had hands and feet, Thurston vowed the adventure would continue.

Eyeballs peered from behind cracked windows as towns-people gawked at the tramp bounding down their street. The people blinked and rubbed their eyes and hoped that this ghoul would disappear. But he did not. He hammered away with his feet, each step faster and louder, and he wailed, "Where is my backpack?" again and again. No one yelled back.

A small, lard boy peered through a ripped corner of the blinds and watched as the half-starved menace screamed about a missing backpack. "What is all that noise," his equally rotund mother yelled from the kitchen. She whisked batter and fiddled with her phone.

"A guy's gone cuckoo bananas." The boy said. He stood and stared through the peephole in the front door. He was as wide as he was short. His body filled with ice cream and cake bloated out of his little, fat face. His beady eyes darted from the kitchen back to the screaming man.

"Is he okay? I can call somebody." The mother offered. She finally turned her attention fully to her son.

The boy lugged his terrible body toward the couch and plopped down. He shrugged but said nothing aloud and turned the television volume up, but it did little to drown the hard consonants in "backpack."

"I'm going to call CJ and let him know the crazies are out." The mother continued.

CJ was the fat kid's older brother. He was taller and thinner than his kid brother, but not due to a strict diet and regimen.

Equally strange but more unhealthy habits had shaped his body. He considered himself a vegetarian but disliked most vegetables and survived off of cheese pizza and leftovers. He poured over fitness magazines and took notes but wouldn't dare lift weights because he wanted to stay svelte. His chest and shoulders were covered in tattoos, and on one arm was a tribal sleeve that followed up his shoulder and surrounded the nape of his neck. A small heart tattoo was etched near his eye. He was thin but surprisingly not frail. A junkyard, tough guy.

His little, chubby brother waited every day for CJ to come home and eagerly hung on to every word. Luckily, CJ never failed to deliver. Every single day, someone wronged him, or he stood up for the honor of a grandma, or a cute girl gave him her number. And every day, the boy loved his brother no matter how obviously tall the tales became.

The boy knew his brother was a tough guy and a noble defender of those who needed protection, but he worried that the wild schizoid that weaved back and forth on the street would clobber CJ. The lunatic had a seven-foot reach and terrifying ghost eyes; CJ wouldn't stand a chance.

Back on the street, Thurston's screams kept the stray cats quiet, and the birds refused to fly. He picked up a rock and skipped it down the double yellow line. As much as he wanted the trip to continue, reality pushed its way to the front of his mind. The adventure floated away with the backpack, and God knew where it had ended. Thurston begrudgingly agreed that it was time to shower, lick his wounds, and head back home. He made his way toward a brightly lit neon Vacancy sign.

Stickers from breweries and bands covered the entrance of the small hotel. Thurston stuck his pimpled and grease-covered head into the doorway and sang, "Good afternoon." CJ grimaced and looked up at the tall skeleton. "What are your nightly rates?" The skeleton grinned.

"We're twenty dollars a night. Showers are five, and towels are five." CJ said. He went back to his desktop and scrolled.

Thurston breathed deep and held it for a few seconds, his wallet tucked neatly inside his stolen backpack. "Would you accept PayPal?"

CJ looked toward the clock. His shift ended fifteen minutes before, and there was no doubt that this was the ghoul that his mother had just warned him about. "Look, man, it's been pretty slow. Why don't you go have a shower on the house?" He returned to the counter, holding a towel with his tribal tattooed hand. "We'll discuss payments and shit after you clean up."

Thurston grabbed the towel and bowed toward CJ. Signs indicated the guest rooms, showers, and laundry room. The shower was pink and small. In the corner stood a wooden stool. Thurston sat and slowly removed his shoes and socks. His socks were hardened from sweat and mud and cocooned around his blistered and bloody toes. As he pulled at the sock, a toenail tore upward, and he winced. He breathed short and rapid breaths as he removed the toenail and set it on the sink. He pulled his shirt up and over his head and took a deep survey of the pitted remains of his body.

The skin around his forehead felt tight and dry, and the closer he leaned into the mirror, the more distorted and disfig-ured his face became. A maze of pimples and the arch of male pattern baldness accentuated his unkempt beard. Thurston covered his hairline and beard with his hand and saw himself. He removed his hands and saw a vagrant lunatic. A young man searching for life sat inside a smelly, malnourished monstrosity.

CJ's replacement was forty-five minutes late. He called his mother back and confirmed that not only had he seen the lunatic but that he was going to be staying at the hostel. The hostel was empty except Thurston, but CJ still made his nightly rounds. The patio chairs were stacked next to the door, and the towels were folded. For CJ, being back in Nowheresville meant that life was a constant fight against boredom. Weekends were spent drinking and walking around Walmart. This odd stranger intrigued him and was a welcome respite from the boredom.

The tall, thin Thurston crept into the lobby. His hair brushed to the side, and his beard tucked against his face. He sauntered toward CJ with a large smile. "I can't pay you. But if you let me use your phone, I could have money for you. Double or triple the nightly rate, and I'll pay that to you directly. And if you help me find a Greyhound tomorrow, I'll pay you even more."

CJ considered telling the clean vagrant to leave. But nothing of note ever happened at a cheap hostel in a worthless town. He tapped his tattoo-covered hand on the counter. "Here's the thing, man, I don't get paid enough to really give a fuck about this place. Where is it you're going? I can give you a ride to the bus station in the morning."

Thurston thanked him and bowed again. "Do you happen to have anything to eat? The last few days have been rough." Thurston rubbed his stomach and mimicked expulsion with his other hand.

CJ rolled his eyes in disgust. He upheld one finger and came back with a large bag of chips and set them on the counter. "This whole day is about charity. Think of it as an early Easter present. What are you doing catching a Greyhound? Heading back home?"

Thurston shrugged. Three wooden benches lined the room, and a small basket filled with plastic eggs sat on a tall stack of Reader's Digest in the corner. "Do you get a lot of traffic through here?" Thurston said. He picked up a newspaper from one of the benches and rifled through it.

"Fuck no, man. During the summer, the farmer's markets

and state fairs bring people in. I see three people a week, tops. I wouldn't have seen you today if my bitch ass coworker was here on time." CJ said. He came from behind the desk and plopped down next to Thurston. The bench creaked beneath him.

Thurston explained the entire situation, including Martha, his mother, his undying need for adventure. He explained the lonely walk and the faux cheese and preserved meats and the irritable bowels that placed him within reach of a thief and ultimately brought him to the hostel's doormat.

CJ listened and nodded. The young man before him lacked discipline. "We've all run into problems on the road. I've hitchhiked out of here three or four times already. Let me tell you something, though. You've been gone a few months, right?"

Thurston nodded.

"Well then, you're already gone, man. If you think life was miserable before, now you get to go back as a failure, and I can promise you, nothing back home has changed. You haven't been gone long enough for anything about you to have changed, either. What's really happened? Sleeping outside and being hungry isn't as bad as going back to a place where people disrespect you. You're already out here, might as well see where it ends up," CJ said.

Thurston flicked at the newspaper. CJ may have been onto something, although Thurston doubted that the innkeeper could've imagined the anguish felt next to the toilet tree. "My phone and all my money are gone. I can't hang around here hoping for my life to change. No offense."

"You're overthinking it. You've lived more in the last six months than you have your whole life. Where was it that you were headed?"

"Colorado."

"Word." CJ said. "I actually know a guy out in Colorado. He runs an outfit called Medary Construction out of Idlewild. I could call him and see if he needs more help for the summer. I owe him a little money, and I could offer that you work to pay it off. You'd be paying me off for the bus ticket, and I'd be paying him off. I can get you a ticket to Denver in the morning. I'll even bring you some clothes and a new backpack with some old camping supplies, too."

Thurston couldn't believe the generosity. Here stood a young man that wandered and adventured successfully. He felt envious of his confidence and hoped that some would rub off on him. "I appreciate it, brother," Thurston said. He stretched his fist out and waved it a bit for CJ to bump it. The trip was back on.

CHAPTER TEN

THE SEATS RUMBLED IN ANTICIPATION. OLD MEN IN rabbit fur-lined bomber hats talked at young women in protest shirts, and a group of foul-smelling ruffians lined the back wall. They wore a mismatch of biker gear and construction safety clothes, and their small leader, Max Medary, snarled at anyone that looked his way. He organized this assembly or, at the very least, instigated it. A group of protestors stood outside the municipal building with signs that read "Keep Us Here" and "We love Colorado."

Frank Garcia stopped and greeted the protestors. His appointment to sheriff razzed a few of the Idlewild good ol' boys, but he worked hard to get to know every resident so they would feel comfortable calling on him for help. "You guys want to come inside and give your two cents?" He asked the group of protesters and held the door open.

"There's not enough room near the exit. If you catch my drift," the old hippie woman with the 'We love Colorado' sign said. Frank peered inside and saw Max and his goons leering near the door. He counted three bruisers, wee Max, and one son of a bitch; perhaps a little too much rough and tumble for one officer to handle, he thought.

"I see. Well, if you change your mind, I'll be standing near the back. I want to be able to keep an eye on everyone." He said and winked at the old hippie. He pulled the door open and sauntered inside. Frank walked straight to Max's spot and stood next to him. "Good evenin', gentlemen."

"We'll see," Max said. He widened his stance and grimaced. His blonde, thin eyebrows seemed non-existent on his face, but they were scrunched in anger.

The mayor, a rotund, white-haired man, stood and marched to the podium, a stack of papers in hand. "Hello, all. This is a special session in order to cover the new proposal, which, as of yesterday, has received the required number of signatures. Let's begin." He wiped at his sweaty face with thick, red hands. Each finger looked like an overstuffed sausage ready to burst from its casing. "Before we get into it. I'd like to go over the proposal outline so that everyone understands what it is that we're talking about. Because I sure as hell don't get it."

And with that, he outlined one of the most preposterous proposals in United States history.

"For those of you who haven't seen this, it begins with a series of complaints against the current General Assembly. I could get into 'em all, but frankly, they come across like the ravings of a loony. However, I'll go ahead and read some of my favorites: environmental laws are crushing industry." The crowd clapped in agreement. The Medary clan hollered, and Officer Garcia waved his hand to quiet them down.

"You're right. Sometimes, it feels like those yahoos in Denver and Boulder have no idea how hard it is to make a living up here. None of them work in mining or logging or out on the rigs, but I digress. Where was I?" The mayor fumbled with his glasses and the papers for a second. "The second complaint: the governor is paying to move Mexicans here to undercut our wages. Whoever wrote this proposal, feel free to meet me afterward, and we can discuss the historical map of Mexico."

The crowd's reaction was mixed. A few turned to each other and wondered how the governor was paying for the Mexicans to move. Was he paying for it himself, or was the conspiracy much more vast? Could it go all the way to the top? The Hispanics in the crowd felt White eyes nervously spot them. Frank grimaced as he hoped that the next point was a little less divisive.

"My favorite complaint, and the last I'll share tonight, is that the state government has misappropriated our tax dollars. I really do agree with this one, even as a member of the government. I have a little more insight than some of you and think it's just great. Now, these complaints get a lot more outlandish and frankly a tad redundant, but what tickles me about the last one I shared is the ideas that the writer has to address these complaints. Idea number one: Build a wall around Meeker County and charge an entrance fee for every vehicle. How will we pay for it without taxes? I'm not sure. Somebody didn't think this all the way through."

Max Medary's face reddened. His fists balled up. Frank noticed the tension and asked him in a low whisper. "You doing alright, bud?"

"There's a lot more in the proposal that the mayor's not saying," Max said through his teeth.

"You think so?" Frank said.

The mayor's microphone gave feedback before he continued. "The second idea is perhaps less taxing but also more outrageous in a way. Meeker County secedes from Colorado and establishes the state of Meeker."

A hush fell over the crowd. The old hippie woman had snuck in during the chaos of the Mexican complaint and held up her sign. "We love living in Colorado," she announced to the townspeople.

"Well, and that's basically the point of the whole proposal. The author broke down how it will work and how the new state could generate revenue, etc. Before I have other speakers, I'd like to make two points. The National Park and the Ute National Forest are federally owned and managed and make up the vast majority of our county. I'm not sure if the federal government will let this plan work out. Secondly, the town of Idlewild's biggest employer is the hospitality industry. Shoot, Elk's View Lodge alone hires damn near two hundred seasonal staff, isn't that right Carol?" The mayor motioned to a small middle-aged woman in the crowd.

"About that. Some years, we have to hire more." She shrugged.

"So this proposal will screw us out of more than two hundred jobs. Okay, that's all my griping. As I said, this has received the amount of signatures needed to have this meeting. And I'd like to invite the author up to answer any questions. Max, do you want to come up to the podium for a moment?"

Bow-legged Max walked in his wide stance toward the podium. He stared at the mayor as he approached and gave a little nod. "Thank you, mayor, for that fine introduction. I appreciate being represented in such an honest and fair way." Max said. He turned his gaze toward the crowd. "Yes, I wrote the proposal. Most of you know that because most of you signed it. Trout and I were there for every one of your signatures."

Trout towered in the back of the room next to Officer

Garcia and gave a wave to the crowd. Carol looked back and hoped that he noticed her but promptly returned to face the front when he didn't. Her cheeks were flushed. She first was attracted to Trout the day she saw him ice fishing on Lily Lake. His large beard covered in ice, he stood outside shirtless in the snow and looked like a handsome, scary Viking. She turned back and looked one more time toward Trout with a slight smile, and again, he looked straight past her. Her face dropped in rejection.

"Now, I don't want to speak for you all, but I, for one, feel pretty stupid. I wonder if the mayor hadn't described the proposal in the way that he had if we'd all feel differently." Max said. His face was the color of a beet. His jaw clenched with every word, and the words came out hard.

"Well, wait just a minute..." the mayor began from his seat.

"I have the podium, Mr. Mayor," Max said. Officer Garcia caught the mayor's eye and slowly skirted along the outside of the room to be closer to the podium. "I don't like feeling stupid. I know you all don't like being seen as stupid. And I know you all don't like the fact that two counties dictate every goddamn thing in this state. I'm of half a mind to burn this whole building to the ground. What do you all think?" Trout and the rest of the safety-vested bikers exited the building. Frank noticed their sudden departure and walked briskly toward the podium.

"Max, let's go outside and have a chat." He said. He thought about his gun, which, at that moment, lay on the floor of his patrol car... three blocks away.

"Absolutely, officer. I'm complying. Everyone sees that, right? I'm being arrested for voicing my opinion. I thought this was America." Max snarled and growled every word. His small hand gripped a knife tightly inside his pocket.

Back up at the podium, the mayor raised his hand to bring a

hush over the crowd. "Now, that was a little too much excitement." The mayor said with his hands still up to quiet the room. Sweat rolled from his head and pooled neatly along his third chin. "There will be a follow-up meeting Tuesday to discuss this further. In the meantime, everyone have a nice evening, and the full proposal will be available on the town website." The mayor shuffled from the podium and greeted his constituents with hugs and reminders of the upcoming election.

Outside, Officer Frank walked Max over to his truck. Trout and the other grunts congregated around the truck. Tobacco spittle ran down Trout's chin. "Are we good?" he asked the cop.

"Quit the act. You know I'm not arresting you. You can't say shit like that in front of people. You know that," Frank said and nudged Max on the shoulder.

"Yeah, yeah." Max said. His head down. The redness and anger cooled with the crisp mountain air. Bowman Peak, the largest mountain in the area, glowed red with alpenglow as the sun set.

Frank glanced at the others in the group. Trout was by far the largest man that he had ever arrested. A drunk and disorderly call led to a smashed window in downtown Idlewild. The two tussled at first, but Frank was able to coax him into the back of the patrol car. He apologized to the tourists that sat on the front deck of that restaurant and joked that Trout was typically as nice as a kitten. The other men he knew but only by reputation. They were mean and ugly, each meaner and uglier than the last, which led to Max. Max and Frank grew up together in Idlewild. As Frank's desire to be a cop grew, Max's desire to be a shithead grew, and he ended up in juvenile detention before he left middle school. When he returned in high school, he was mean and wanted to fight everyone.

"Look, guys. I don't really give a shit about your anti-taxation plan, or whatever it is you think you're cooking up. Just don't get the whole damned town riled up for no reason. There are ways to do things, and tonight was not the way. I'll talk to the mayor, and when we have the meeting on Tuesday, I'll be sure to have him be a little more fair, and you guys work on your damn tempers. Deal?" Frank said. He offered a handshake to Max.

Max thought for a moment and conceded to the handshake.

"You boys drive safe." Frank smacked the hood of the work truck and walked back toward his patrol car.

After a few moments of watching him walk away, Max broke the silence. "Well, that went well." The gang laughed and took turns slapping each other's backs.

"You sure are funny," Trout said. His eyes welled in tears from the laughter. "I thought you were really mad for a minute."

"Oh, I was furious. That mayor really chaps my ass, but he made it so easy. I'll go to every town meeting and say the same thing. If we can get the proposal on the ballot, we can get everyone to vote for it. Just like we got them to sign it in the first place." Max said. Trout nodded in agreement.

The men piled in the cab of the pickup. Their shoulders smashed into each other as they squeezed in. "Which of you wants to go to Denver to pick that kid up?"

Trout looked at Max perplexed.

"The kid from back east?" Max reminded the group.

Trout shrugged.

"CJ called about there being a drifter who needed some cash to get out here. I told him that I'd send him the money for the bus ticket and that the kid could work off that debt and CJ's debt, too. Summer's here, and we got a lot of projects coming up. Plus our special project," Max explained.

Trout nodded and said, "Oh yeah, the kid. And the special project. I didn't forget."

"I know you didn't. And because you didn't forget, you and Corky can head down to Denver to get him. Isn't that right?"

Corky slapped his leg, and an exaggerated frown crept across his face.

"You've got it, boss," Trout said.

CHAPTER ELEVEN

THE WOMEN PILED IN ONE AFTER ANOTHER. THE COFFEE shop was suited for twelve people to sit comfortably and three or four to stand in line, and, including baristas, it could fit twenty people maximum. The planning committee for the women's retreat was thirty-four full-sized women. Each wore heavy, starched shirts that only irritated them further as they sweat from being so tightly packed in.

"I have no interest in going to Colorado. It's a vile place for homosexuals and weed freaks," a small-mouthed woman with a yellow scarf spoke up. The barista sighed when she overheard the comment. These were overtime hours, and no amount of extra chairs seemed to accommodate the large crowd. She hoped that each woman had at least an inch of table to set their coffee upon.

"It's the same story in every church. The young guns come in, fresh out of seminary, and try to worm their way into a community," the youngest of the women said. Her chin wobbled a few precarious seconds after she spoke. She straightened herself out and huffed at the audacity of the situation.

Anna and Dottie surveyed the room. Dottie knew that the women would sway to whatever Anna decided; there had been many women's ministry decisions that fell upon her. Anna looked around to see if anyone was happy. The Gail Country Club was luxurious to these women, and they felt as if the one thing that they had was being stripped from them. Revolt was in the air.

Anna wished Dottie would give her some guidance. But Dottie didn't seem to notice the telepathic waves shooting from Anna's eyeballs and looked disgusted at every whine and complaint that erupted from the peanut gallery.

"Ladies, ladies. I agree that Pastor Doug may not be as well suited for the church as some of the previous leaders, but that is just because he is young. When's the last time we had someone in their forties want to be our pastor? I certainly remember the leadership being walking corpses when I was a younger," She began. The group quieted down and adjusted themselves to see Anna. The barista took a big, deep breath and slid against the wall until she sat on the floor. Her vertebrate anatomy flashcards sat in a pile next to her and the animosity in the room made her want to hide for the rest of the day and give up on studying completely. Perhaps she'd just run away.

"The Country Club is great; I'll be the first to admit that. But change can be a good thing. When my husband first started working in Toronto, people would tell him that children don't need their own programming. Did he listen? No, he refused to listen to anyone, especially me. And his show, Bertha's Town, was the highest-rated puppet-based children's program for the five to seven demographic in 1972. Would he have succeeded at that if he listened?" She paused for a moment and eyed the crowd. Each woman seemed to turn to the other and shrug as if to say, 'How should we know?'

The moment had gone a beat too long because when Anna

spoke again, she had forgotten where she was in her grand speech. "Oh, oh my. I think I've lost my train of thought," Anna said. She turned toward Dottie for guidance. Dottie shrugged at her and went back to sipping at her coffee. "But that's my point. We don't need Pastor Doug to tell us that Colorado will be fun, we all know it will be. We all deserve to get up in the mountains and take some time for ourselves."

The women searched between themselves to find the point. The young woman with the wobble chin clapped, and the rest of the group joined in. "How will we do it?" A small, elderly brunette asked. She pushed her glasses up, but they quickly slid back down to the tip of her nose.

"That's the point of this meeting," Dottie said. She stood up from her comfortable seat. The doorbell jingled as a college student with a big computer bag came in. He saw the large group of women sprawled all over the room, turned around, and walked right back out the door.

"We don't bite." One of the women called out.

"We will have a car wash," Dottie explained and suggested that Anna sit down. Anna thanked her with a whisper and collapsed in the chair beside Dottie. "The bake sale doesn't bring in enough customers, and I don't want to try and raise money just with donations alone. We will have a carwash with a 'donations encouraged' sign. We need to raise another thirty thousand dollars to be able to do this trip with everyone."

The room fell silent. It was the first time that a dollar amount had been uttered to the group. It seemed like an astronomical price for a weekend trip for some fun, especially fun that some of the ladies wouldn't be able to enjoy, and the idea of using the Country Club appealed to them all. There were club sandwiches and funny umbrellas that the bartenders used for the drinks, and an Applebee's was right down the block. The idea of a big trip out of state daunted the group.

"I think Dottie's idea is brilliant. I'll go ahead and gather the supplies, and we hope to see everyone at the car wash. It will be a doozy," Anna exclaimed. The group cheered again and shuffled out the door, one small shuffle step at a time.

Before Anna could follow the small, old woman parade out of the cafe, Dottie tapped her on the shoulder. "Will you hang back with me for a moment? I want to ask you something."

"Of course," Anna said. She loved her friend.

Dottie took a sip of her tea and looked out the window at the group of geriatrics. She shook her head. "These women can't wash cars, Anna."

Anna turned to look out the window herself. "Of course, they can. How else will we raise money? The carwash was your idea."

"I think you should pay for the trip," Dottie said. There was not a hint of hesitation or sarcasm. She knew that Anna could afford to pay for the group.

"Now, Dottie." Anna began to protest. How could she possibly be responsible for the enjoyment of the whole women's ministry? There seemed to be a lack of concern from the rest of the women that Anna would figure out how to make it all work out, and she certainly didn't want to cater to these lazy whims.

"It will mean a lot to them, and it's the nice, Christian thing to do," Dottie said, and she was right.

Anna sighed and took a deep breath. "Well, I always want to be a nice, Christian woman. But don't let anyone know that I was the one that paid for it. I don't want to be seen as a charity."

"I won't say a word," Dottie said.

CHAPTER TWELVE

AVERY PULLED MAGNUS TOWARD THE CAR AND TOSSED HER
bag into the backseat. "There are so many places in America
that we can go to help pull you out of your spiritual crisis. Santa
Fe, Joshua Tree, New Orleans. I think that we should pick a
direction and drive. We'll drive until we find something that
piques your interest. That scratches your soul itch."

Magnus looked across the street and then turned his head
and looked the other way. He rubbed his chin for a second and
said. "Let's head west then. Everyone says head west."

Avery slapped the hood of the car and hollered. "This is
going to be fun."

"Don't forget, I'll need more of my green juice before we get
on the road," Magnus said.

Avery rolled her eyes. "I've packed two weeks' worth. Are
you sure that your stomach can handle green juice and
driving?"

"Positive."

It wasn't long after they were on the road that Magnus's

stomach gurgled in the passenger seat. "I'm always impressed by your sweetness, Avery," he said. Magnus rolled his head to look at her. Bits of green juice and undigested celery spotted his chin, and his breath smelled rancid. "If God told me that you were an angel, I would not argue."

Thankfully for Magnus, Avery mapped out every truck and rest stop and counted down aloud as the mileage dropped. "We've got fifty miles until the next bathroom." After twenty minutes of driving, she made another announcement, "Now thirty." And with each update, Magnus looked out the window and rested his head back against the glass. An oily spot grew with each smear.

The two-mile mark to the exit approached. "Are you absolutely sure that you don't want to stop?"

"I do not need to stop at every bathroom opportunity like a child. What do you think I am, an eighty-year-old man with a bladder the size of a pea?" He huffed and crossed his arms. The love he had for her earlier completely replaced it with irritation. Irritable bowels and an irritable man. The car sped along the highway until the final exit sign came into sight. "Well, you know if you need to go, we can stop."

"I don't need to go," Avery said.

"Hang on for just a minute. Maybe a snack would be a good idea." Magnus pleaded. Sweat dripped from his forehead as the nausea took hold.

"I'm not hungry," She said. She turned toward him and smiled. "Thank you, though."

"Avery, I know what you're doing. We have to stop. You know we have to stop." Magnus's hand gripped the door handle tightly. His knuckles white with fear.

"I thought you weren't eighty," Avery said.

"Avery, for the love of all things Holy, we need to pull over.

This is a battle of life and death. I don't want to puke in this car." Magnus said. His voice was a high-pitched squeal.

Avery took the exit, and Magnus hopped out and ran inside. After a few minutes, he came back out and plopped down in the passenger seat. He pulled out his green juice and took a large gulp. He wiped at his mouth and tilted the tumbler toward Avery to offer her a swig. The cleanse failed to cleanse his soul but succeeded in cleansing his esophagus and seemed to heighten his lucidity, especially after a binge and purge cycle.

"I think it's time I come clean." He proclaimed. Full of the lucidity brought by an empty stomach. "I'm not a businessman, at least not really. I want to be. I want to have the answers and make the right choices. But I haven't. My parents founded the company. I have not done anything on my own. My mom is on the board and oversees decisions, and frankly, it's a lot of work to seem like an entrepreneur. I've vomited six times today. I have hemorrhoids the size of the Brooklyn Bridge. And guess what? No one can see me torturing myself. So why am I doing this?" Magnus looked out toward the highway. The road carried on forever. "I think I'm just going to make yogurt smoothies and dye them green. No one will know the difference."

"If we stay on the interstate, there'll be a truck stop every hundred miles," Avery said.

"Thank you," Magnus replied. He rested his head back on the window.

Avery pulled the car slowly back onto the highway. She reveled in every aspect of the road trip. It was her first long haul trip and her first time seeing the 'real America.' Her life up to that point had consisted of staff cooking and setting the table, a maid service to do laundry, and a driver to take her around town. When she moved away, she realized that she'd never done laundry before and there was a lifetime of chores to learn.

She looked out of the side of her eye toward Magnus. He shook and grew sicker. She did not understand the need to be seen as something that he obviously wasn't. Any amount of fondness for him was growing into disdain. She knew Magnus's thoughts were phony. His laugh and voice and the way he styled his hair: all false. But he refused to be less. Against all sense, he did not admit to anyone else it was all fake.

The only reality that made sense for his extreme roller-coaster of emotionality was addiction. Magnus quaked when not given attention. He craved it. He couldn't resolve reality from his own thoughts, and every time he was granted clarity, he hated that clear picture of himself and his lack of convictions. He stared out the window. And besides all that, the green juice was not filling. Each cloud grew and shrank, and Magnus watched as the sky transformed from cumulus to hamburgers and stratus to fries. His head pressed firmly against the glass as he knew that the river ran cold with Coca-Cola, and each boat launch was equipped with long straws.

"Avery, I have realized that I am too weak to continue. I am truly no one. I have not a single thought or care that will impact anyone, and I must die now." Magnus sighed and moved his heavy head from the glass, resting it in his hands.

The car screeched to a stop as Avery pushed the brakes with both feet. The backend fishtailed slightly into traffic. "I don't care that you're nuts. This is the first time you have a truly good idea. Becoming a better person, even if you're going about, it in such a tremendously stupid way, is the best idea you've ever had. And I am so tired of being dragged around by your whims. We are going to finish this road trip, and maybe you can think of a way to fill your time. Give a Ted talk or something, for Christ's sake. It will be filled with people excited to talk to you about tech and your pursuit of self-discovery. And who knows, maybe by then, you will have actually learned something profound about yourself. Until then, stop drinking the damn green juice, eat food, and help me look for the biggest ball of twine in Minnesota." Avery said. She reached into her jacket pocket and tossed a granola bar in Magnus's lap.

"This is wonderful. I always have my best ideas after eating."

CHAPTER THIRTEEN

AVERY HAD LONG HARBORED THE SUSPICION THAT, unbeknownst to the world, her boss was an idiot. Three days before, this realization would have elicited an ill feeling of fear. Maybe she would have called her grandpa for advice or quit unexpectedly and vowed to never speak of her time at Onyx again. But as she drove and listened to the inane utterances that seemed to erupt from Magnus, the realization was easy to swallow. The only aspect of it that she still didn't quite grasp was how on earth he ended up being the founder of such an influential app.

The scenarios she played in her head made her feel a bit like a misandrist. How else could anyone explain that a man, who is so incapable, is in charge of, and makes, so much money? When she was in college, she used Onyx to send very explicit messages to her then-boyfriend, and now she knew that those messages lived on in perpetuity within the confines of a warehouse filled with offsite servers somewhere deep within the San Fernando Valley.

She felt the need to be exceedingly patient: patient with herself, as this was a decent enough job, and she could always use it as a steppingstone toward a more fulfilling career. Patient with Magnus because he needed tender care and ever-constant kiddie gloves. And exceedingly patient with every person who felt the need to explain to her their very specific and personal reasons for thinking that Magnus was either a saint or a bastard. She usually could agree with the latter.

But that was the position that she was currently in, standing on the shoulder of a highway in northern Wyoming, next to a Wildlife Corridor sign and a large canyon. The pull-off had at least thirty-five people, all standing packed together, as they peered down the canyon. Magnus had seen the large crowd before he realized it was a designated wildlife viewing area and had insisted that they stop. "A road trip is meant for spontaneity," he exclaimed. He reached across the car to the wheel and yanked it hard to the shoulder. Luckily, Avery had kept both hands tight around the wheel for such exclamations and pulled the car gently over.

"I knew it was going to be something worthwhile. Usually, things are quite wonderful for me," Magnus exclaimed again as he noticed the large Wildlife Corridor sign. It read that Bighorn Sheep are native to Wyoming, and despite competition from humans, invasive species, and agriculture, they thrive in this particular canyon. Magnus read the sign carefully. "We're looking for sheep, Avery."

She nodded along and muttered, "Idiot," beneath her breath. It worried her that she had once admired this man, and it disgusted her that she had at one time found him attractive. "Do you want your green juice?" She said loud enough for him to hear.

"Of course not. I'm already firing on all cylinders today." He shouted back to her from the sign. Each of the other thirty-five people standing within earshot looked at the pair of them and their Mercedes. Avery watched from beside the car as Magnus wormed his way through the crowd and ended up right next to the cliffside. "Where should I be looking?" He asked aloud to no one in particular.

An old woman with an Audubon Society shirt and a wide-brimmed hat replied, "We're looking at raptors. About thirty feet down the other side of the cliff."

Magnus's face twisted with uncertainty. "But this is the viewing area for Bighorn Sheep."

The old woman turned to him again. This time, she kept her binoculars tight against her face. "The sheep don't come back to this elevation until a little later in the year. They're still in the spring grazing pastures down in the valley."

"Of course they are." Magnus sighed. He threw his hands up in defeat and kicked rocks while he shuffled back to the car. "Let's go," he said to Avery.

"You don't want to stay and look at the birds?" She asked. Magnus shook his head and feigned a yawn. They both got back into the car, but before she put it into reverse, she saw three teenage boys sitting on the hood of the car next to them, and all three stared at Onyx with glee. "Those boys are looking at your app."

"And? Lots of people use Onyx every day. It's actually what marketing is focused on now: 'How can we be of assistance today?'" Magnus said. He stared out the passenger window for a moment. "It would be interesting to hear what people think of the app, in a real-world scenario, I mean."

"I agree. Do you want to go talk to them?" But before Avery could finish her thought, Magnus opened the car door and approached the three teenagers. She couldn't quite make out what was being said. But Magnus was on display. He motioned with his hands and smiled intensely. He seemed to be pointing to the cliff again and again. The boys laughed, and Magnus walked over to the cliffside. He sat down on the barrier wall and took his shoes off; the boys were still in hysterics. One boy live-streamed with the Onyx app. Then Magnus stood and took a step up onto the barrier wall.

Avery leaped out of the car. "Hey! What are you doing? Magnus. Look at me." She yelled at him and ran over to the wall. She knew that if she lunged at him that he may fall, so she kept her distance and took careful steps forward. "Magnus. What are you doing?" She said again, but this time in a hushed tone. The boys laughed behind her.

"They hate me," Magnus said.

"They don't hate you. What did they say?"

"Those miscreants said that the only thing they use Onyx for is to have something stupid to look at while they shit. They look at shit while they shit. That's what they said." A tear rolled down Magnus's cheek. He lowered himself onto the ledge and let his feet dangle off. He kicked his legs like a toddler in a highchair.

Avery took a small step toward the sniveling, pathetic man. What could she do but try to calm him down and bring him back to reality, if he was even capable of arriving safely back in reality. Had he ever really lived within the confines of reality? For a brief, fleeting second, she considered tripping as she approached and landing into him, giving him that final courageous shove he needed to end it all. To finally help Magnus escape the mundane and nightmarish existence he found himself trapped in.

She thought better of it and didn't push him.

"Get on with it already." One of the boys cried out. The

excitement of a possible death soured as the moments turned to minutes, and each boy returned back to their phones and mindless scrolling.

"Magnus," Avey said in a low, soft voice. She spoke to him in the same tone that she used for her cat, not a trace of aggression but a hint of a secret treat that she may or may not have in her hand behind her back. Of course, she didn't have a treat for Magnus, but she did have the ability to promise him a treat if he came down. "I booked you a lecture."

Even at a whisper, the words took up space around Magnus. His legs stopped swinging. He looked up toward her with large crocodile tears on their way down his face. "You did?"

"Yes, and everyone is very excited to hear you speak about Onyx," Avery said. Not one ticket had been purchased for the event. The bird people seemed to become bored with the raptors and left one at a time.

"Okay, I guess suicide can wait until after that," Magnus said. Avery rolled her eyes and held out her hand to help Magnus turn around and step back down from the ledge. "Did you hear me? I can just commit suicide after the event. It will be dependent on everyone's reaction to my lecture. Maybe they'll love me and everything will be fine."

"Let's not get our hopes up," Avery whispered under her breath, but loud enough for him to hear, she said, "I am sure it'll be great."

As Avery and Magnus made their way back to the car, her heart rate slowly coming back down to normal, she scowled at the boys and considered giving them each a hard whack alongside their heads. There were plenty of reasons to be cruel to Magnus, but those boys didn't know that.

There was no way to tell the magnitude of Magnus's feelings or if they were based in reality at all. There seemed to be a very distinct divorce between reality and life, and Magnus existed somewhere in that ether, and that scared Avery. All she could hope to do was get further down the road and wait for his mood of elated narcissism to come back. It was her job to temper both his self-loathing and self-importance. Perhaps, on the road, she'd be able to find that balance for Magnus.

CHAPTER FOURTEEN

THE PAIR OF RUFFIANS RACED DOWN THE CANYON. TROUT drove the dilapidated 1986 Toyota with ferocity, and Corky spit into his empty Mountain Dew bottle. The spit from his right cheek was from chewing tobacco, and when he spit from the left side of his mouth it was sunflower seeds. The trick was to swallow the seed without swallowing any of the tobacco and spit out the seed exterior without spitting out any of the tobacco. He failed consistently at both. And as one might guess, his stomach churned between the layer of tobacco and the quick pace of going down the winding canyon.

"Do you know where we're going?" Corky managed, his face a sickly green. He hung his head out the window and took a deep breath to try and control his tobacco-flavored upsick.

"The bus station." Trout declared. His eyes never ventured from the road ahead.

Queen City bus station sat at the crossroads of Broadway and 12th Street in downtown Denver. Creeps and homeless people and their makeshift tents lined the streets. The entire area from Coors Field to the state capitol building reeked of urine. It was a menagerie of the worst Colorado had to offer: politicians, bankers, and venture capitalists. They sneered at the homeless, or worse, ignored them, or even worse still, made fun of them, without any indication that who they were making fun of was, in fact, a person. Thurston felt uneasy as the bus pulled into the station.

Denver was the first city Thurston had encountered in what felt like ages. He slept most of the way and missed hundreds of miles of corn fields. He rubbed his eyes at the brightness of the city. It reflected off all the glass and steel and fell directly into his eyes. There were bums and ironic mustaches and hippies and suits, and Thurston wasn't sure where he fit in among the crowd. He saw a group of young people, slightly older than him, in fleece sweaters with company logos embroidered and decided to stand near them.

As Thurston walked toward the group of sweaters, the backfire from the Toyota carrying Trout and Corky startled him. He looked back toward it and noticed the words Medary Construction, Idlewild, CO on the side of the door and a Free State of Meeker bumper sticker. He hoped that the two men didn't see him as he ducked behind the crowd of tech bros.

"Have you heard about the Meeker movement?" The tallest fleece vest asked and motioned toward the old pickup. His hairline begged to be put down, but he brushed it to the side and hoped that no one noticed.

"No, what's that?" An Asian vest asked.

"These hicks and rednecks up near Idlewild want to secede and create the state of Meeker. The funniest thing about it is that they want to build a wall and charge people entry fees." The tall fleece explained. The group laughed in unison, and their various logos bobbed with glee.

"I guess we won't rent a cabin there this year." The only female vest complained. She rolled her eyes, and the rest of the group rolled theirs in agreement. "They know that tourism is the only thing they have, right?"

Thurston realized that he had hidden behind the wrong group as they began to eye the seemingly homeless young man. He backed up to find another crowd that was better suited to his peculiarities and found himself backed into a wheelchair.

"Excuse me." The man in the wheelchair exclaimed.

Thurston jumped and apologized. "I didn't see you there."

"Sure, you didn't." The man huffed. He wore a pink cowboy hat and matching pink rhinestone-encrusted boots. A small Chihuahua mutt sat on his lap and yapped at Thurston. "Are you lost?" The man asked

Thurston thought for a moment. He was in Denver at the Queen City bus station. He was headed to Idlewild to work at Max Medary's construction company but had thought better of it now that he was in Denver. The words failed to form coherent sentences, and Thurston answered without explanation. "Yes. I'm trying to get to Idlewild."

"Oh, honey. Why you headed up there? It's still snowing and cold." The man shivered and held the dog close. "You'll die up there for sure."

"I'm supposed to work around Idlewild for the summer. The company paid for my bus ticket out west as long as I promised to work off the debt." Thurston said. He looked for the ratty old work truck and was undecided on what he was going to do.

"So, you're a slave." The man eyed Thurston up and down. "That's a big problem for you, but good luck." The man said and rolled his wheelchair away from Thurston.

"What do you mean I'm a slave? Hey wait." Thurston chased the man and caught up with him quickly. "It's just paying off a debt for a friend and the bus ticket. No big deal. I want to be here or at least in the mountains. There's a lot more action there than back home."

The man ignored Thurston and rolled through the cross-walk to the other side. Across another intersection was Colfax. Once they reached the other side of the road, Thurston stood in front of the wheelchair. "Hey, I'm obviously not from around here. Maybe you could show me some sights while I wait for my ride. Or you could give me a ride to Idlewild, and I could just explain to my employer once I get there. I don't have any money, but I could pay you back for the gas once I start getting paychecks again."

"Ha!" The man spit at Thurston. The dog danced in a little circle and found a new, more comfortable spot to lay. "You going to pay me after you pay two other guys? Uh-huh. I'm not looking to give out charity. Also, I can't drive. I don't know if you failed to see what's in front of you, but my legs do not work. I don't even have a car. Shit."

Thurston understood and felt a little silly suggesting that a paraplegic drive him. The man wheeled off, and Thurston stood frozen in his sheepish mistake. "Wait." He finally said. Thurston caught back up with the wheelchair.

"I'm hungry. If you're hungry, I'd love to pick your brain and get a feel of Denver. I mean, I'm new here. Maybe I will just stay in Denver and not go to Idlewild." Thurston said. People walked around the pair. More vests stared as they assumed the young man was harassing the homeless paraplegic, yet no one stopped to help the situation.

"Okay, I'll get lunch with you. Pete's Kitchen ain't too far from here, and I've got a hookup there, so we can eat for free." The man said and wheeled off down Colfax. Thurston bounded along behind him.

Back in the pickup, Trout and Corky parked next to the bus station. Corky opened the door and dizzily centered himself. The tall high-rises and the swallowed tobacco juice caused him to have vertigo. Ravens noticed and circled high above Corky. The idea of such a large man as a feast caused a frenzy in the bird world.

"What does this kid look like?" Trout asked.

Corky shrugged and threw up next to the truck. He stood and wiped his mouth. "I thought you knew."

"Fuck's sake," Trout said. "We can't really go back home without him."

The pair walked through the throngs of vests, past the hippies, and toward the capitol building. Trout towered over the crowd. His tattooed arms bulged from his sleeves, and the crowd noticed and spread around him. Even the wild-eyed junkies and undercover narcotics officers knew the pair were trouble and bowed out of the way.

Trout burst into a bookstore and looked inside. Then, at the next shop door, Corky peered inside and announced, "I'm looking for a kid," to shrugged shoulders and general disinterest. Trout's outheld phone showed a picture of Thurston, a badly lit, compressed profile picture. "It could be any of these guys," Corky said.

Down Colfax, the pink cowboy waited for Thurston to catch up. Thurston's life on the road, as brief as it was, hadn't prepared him for east Colfax. Head shops and sex stores and hipster cafes in old industrial warehouses pulled Thurston's attention in every direction. He ran into other pedestrians, stepped off the sidewalk, and slammed his head into a pot shop sign.

"You're a mess." The pink cowboy said. Thurston quickened his pace and opened the door to Pete's Kitchen for the man and his dog.

The cafe was small, with a few tables and booths near the kitchen and a sunroom with larger tables. It was a Greek-owned cafe with American-style breakfast and Greek lunch options. Thurston watched the lamb slowly get sliced.

"So what's your deal?" The pink cowboy said. He hid the small dog inside his coat. The only thing visible was the little dog's snout.

"I ran away from home," Thurston said. He took a large sip through his straw for longer than usual. He stared out the window, searching for the two men from the pickup. He felt odd avoiding his responsibilities, especially when they had paid for his ticket. "I guess there was a girl," Thurston explained.

"Oh boy. There's always a girl." The pink man laughed and slapped the table. "Well, they ain't never been a problem for me," he said.

"This was actually the first to cause me problems. I don't even know what happened. It was like one day I woke up, and I was scared of everything. I was scared of rejection, scared of the things that made me happy. I felt like I woke up and began watching life pass me by, and there was nothing I could do to stop it," said Thurston. "I kind of cracked up and found myself on a bus to Denver."

"And you want to go to Idlewild? You like living in Igloos?" The pink cowboy poured half and half into his coffee and made it a muddy tan. The spoon tinged against each side as sugar and honey were added.

"I think I wanted something different. To kind of prove himself. But now that I'm out here, maybe I will just stay in Denver or go up to the mountains and not tell my employer." Before Thurston could elaborate further, two large, mean construction worker types burst in through the front door. One held a phone in front of his face and looked around the room and caught Thurston's gaze. He looked at the phone again and looked back toward Thurston. "Please excuse me," Thurston said. Without thinking, he leaped to his feet and decided he no longer wanted to uphold his end of the bargain. He gathered his backpack and made his way toward the restroom. The two men pushed their way into the cafe.

"Hey, we want to talk to you!" Corky yelled. Thurston refused to turn around and pushed out the back of the restaurant into the alleyway. He ran toward Colfax and headed back past the head shops and sex toy stores and the lesbian bars. He ran past the state capitol and 16th Street mall and the Queen City bus station. Every time he dared to look behind himself, Trout and Corky were a few steps closer.

A bus toward the outskirts of the station began to roll its way onto Broadway. Thurston ran toward it, with arms waving in the air. The bus driver shook his head and pointed at the watch on his arm. He shrugged and mouthed an apology to Thurston. Thurston, in a split-second decision said, "Help me." He banged on the door to the bus, and the driver acquiesced. He threw the bus into park and waited for the boy to board. "I'll pay whatever. Let's just go. Those guys are chasing me." Thurston pointed to the two lumbering giants that wrecked their way down 16th Street Mall.

"Are those cops?" The bus driver asked. There was a twinge of worry in his eye.

"No, if anything, I should call the cops," Thurston explained.

"Fair enough." The driver said and placed the bus back into gear. The doors closed with a jolt, and the bus rolled onto the road. Thurston placed his face against the glass and watched Trout and Corky realize what had happened.

"God damn it," Trout said. "Max is going to be pissed."

"We can always bring him back a little treat from the city. There's a chocolate store we passed a little ways back." Corky tried to reason with the giant.

"I will strangle you." Trout said and thought for a moment.

"But Max would be even more pissed if he's two workers short this summer and not just one."

"Well, that one's long gone," Corky said. He pointed to the sign on the back of the bus: Daily Denver to Cañon City to Denver. "I doubt we need to chase help clear across the country."

The bus was headed for Cañon City, a four-day walk from Idlewild.

CHAPTER FIFTEEN

THURSTON AROSE FROM HIS LATE AFTERNOON NAP AND shook the bus station dust off of himself. This was his sixth month on the road, and all of his romantic notions of vagrancy and authentic living had flitted away with the realization that it's much harder to be an authentic idealist when there's nowhere safe to sleep. However, it had become clear that the true adventurers, those grand climbers and big game hunters and pearl divers, were not the people struggling every day to find a safe place to sleep. Only dentists, lawyers, and trust fund kids seemed to live the life for which Thurston longed.

The strange predicament he found himself in these days was the ebbs and flows of feeling overwhelmingly defeated by his own choices and the ever present hope that he was in charge of his own way. On days when he awoke on bus benches, he felt defeat. On days when the sunrise hung pink along the clouds, he felt hope. And every day had several moments of both. Beautiful creek along his path: hope. Unbelievable smell at the truck stop: defeat. There never seemed to be a safe middle ground.

With the knowledge that in a few hours, perhaps moments, he would be awestruck by the awesomeness of existence, he tried not to dwell too long on the despair of waking up with no adventure in sight or a newfound envy of dentists. He grabbed his rucksack and heaved it onto his back, thankful for CJ's old camping equipment.

He walked through old town Cañon City, past the cafes and sandwich shops, straight toward the mountains. This was the first time since he left that the adventure he needed was within grasp. Of course, he could see the mountains from Denver, but here they were merely steps away. Finally, he thought to himself. This was why he left in the first place.

Thurston didn't bother with a map and instead held CJ's compass tightly in his right hand; it was hard to get lost if you knew where you were going. He vaguely knew that Idlewild was northwest from Cañon City, but he still hadn't fully decided if that was where he wanted to go. In fact, there were mountains near Cañon City that seemed just as wild and large as any in the Idlewild Valley. On the other hand, the National Park was closer to Idlewild, and he wanted to be able to see wilderness as large and as untouched as he could. So he set off with no real plan of going anywhere in particular.

For the first few miles, Thurston followed the highway as it wound through a canyon, but he saw a break in the canyon wall and wanted to bushwhack. The higher mountains were snow-covered, and Thurston wanted to get high up on a ridge line and look out over the endless expanse of higher and higher mountains. Although he walked for hours every day, he struggled to catch his breath. He had never been at elevation, nor had he ever walked up a mountain, and the most direct way up was not doing his legs any favors. With each step, his calf tensed, and it felt like he had a Charley horse. Then he would take a step with the other leg, and the exact same thing happened. He stopped and sat a while and looked back toward the town.

He had risen high enough to see above the treeline, the higher peaks still miles away, but from this vantage point, he could see people going about their days. The mailman smiled as he walked along the main street and waved at each shopkeeper and barista. The bus driver honked lightly and told a group of schoolchildren that it was okay to cross the road. And Thurston sat and saw that life seemed idyllic and peaceful. The thought of staying at Cañon City grew the more he considered it as a nice place to call home.

With his breath caught, Thurston stood and stomped onward. Sweat drenched his back where the sack sat and down the front of his shirt. Instead of heading straight up, he began to walk zig zags, and his legs thanked him. He imagined that near the top, there would be a neat trail along the ridge line that would allow him easy access to the highest peaks. At least he hoped that there would only be minor elevation gain as he headed deeper into the backcountry. But the ridge line never arrived, and the more he walked, the higher the summit and the snow seemed away.

The loose dirt trail was replaced by large boulders the closer Thurston got to the peaks. Each seemed to be larger than the next, and he needed his hands to steady himself as he navigated through the maze of rocks. Looking back down, he could no longer see the town at all, but only the very top of the highest trees, and even they seemed gray and obscured by the distance. The summit continued to get higher, and in the shadows, he saw snow. He placed his hands on a boulder and swiftly hopped over it and landed hard. The excitement of getting closer helped dull the ache in his ankles. The beginning of a small stream came down from a large snowbank, and

Thurston filled his hands with the cold water and splashed it on his face.

Every moment upon the slope, high above the trees, filled Thurston with the boyhood eagerness for life that he hoped would open like a pit in the earth and swallow him whole. The joy of adventure held him in a warm embrace, and he wondered if this was what people felt like when they were in love. He thought about Martha's fingernails and the weird dirt that she would pick out with her teeth. Perhaps he hadn't been in love with Martha.

The summit was coming into view. He saw a large gully of steep snow adorned with rocks on either side of it. He wondered how steep and slippery the rocks must be with the ice and snow melting upon them. He trudged forward. Although Thurston had no way of knowing, the mountain was not a famous Colorado peak, nor was it a particularly interesting obscure hike. It was a day hike for children.

Thurston also didn't realize that the snow gully that he wanted to avoid, the couloir, was the safest path up this particular mountain at this particular time of year. The rocks were slippery, and the other slope was avalanche-prone, but the tightly packed stable snow within the couloir could be walked up or skied down without any worry at all. But none of that mattered to Thurston because, despite wanting to be adventurous, he hadn't made even the slightest effort to prepare for the type of adventures that he wanted. A compass and hand-me-down camping gear were not what was needed for mixed ice and rock climbing.

The rock felt cold through the glove. It was wet and felt loose beneath him as he carefully moved his way upward. His footing was sure, but every time his hand grasped for something more stable, it was met with ice and uncertainty. He managed to get both hands underneath himself and wiggle onto a ledge.

The summit was closer now, and he couldn't wait to bag it and head back down.

A rock moved slightly above, and another realization consumed Thurston; he didn't know what wild animals could be with him at this elevation. A bobcat, a bear, a god damned lion? He had no way of knowing if anything at this height had a taste for man. As he worried and looked about the ledge, a fat brown rodent peered back at him with sleep in its eyes. It yawned and bared its large yellow teeth and crawled back into its hole to try and sleep for another month. Thurston had never considered that there would be high-altitude land beavers, but stranger things had happened.

Maybe it was the fact that he had seen such a cute little woodland creature, or perhaps it was because Thurston had failed to even take the slightest measures while going into the backcountry, but the ground slipped out from underneath him. Although it was only a slight misstep, an accident of the smallest proportions, he began to tumble backward. If he had been in the couloir, it wouldn't have been a disaster at all, and he would have been able to catch himself against the gentle slope. Unfortunately, from this vantage point, he had twenty feet before he landed on the hard-packed snow. He tumbled and tumbled with no knowledge of which way was up or down and no way of knowing how to stop.

Real adventurers, the dentists and lawyers of the world, would have brought ice axes and beacons and, unless extraordinarily bold, a partner. The ice ax would be used against the snow to self-arrest and if buried in snow, the beacon would allow others to find you. Thurston was not extraordinarily bold nor capable of dealing with the harsh reality that this mountain could very well end it for him.

Once he came to a stop, there was no sense of relief or a quick prayer for his good fortune of being alive; he wondered if he had died, if the marmot, the small rodent, would gnaw on him. The thought of the little creature using Thurston as sustenance brought an odd sense of comfort.

Thurston was quite banged up. The metallic taste of blood-filled Thurston's mouth. He winced as he opened his mouth to release his tongue from between his teeth. His ears rang as he sat up. Twenty feet further down the slope was the cliff that he had navigated earlier, and he breathed heavily. This was the adventure he longed for, he thought. He wanted to laugh, but his chest hurt against his jacket. He felt constrained under his own weight.

He wiggled himself gently to see if there was any more give in the snow. He leaned back against the slope and removed his gloves. Thurston traced his finger along his teeth and felt grooves and notches that hadn't existed before. His sore tongue automatically ran itself along the bottom teeth and confirmed several were chipped.

There was a hundred fifty feet between Thurston and the gentle, flatter earth. He put his gloves back on and pushed hard to get to his feet. The soreness already set in as he swayed back and forth and hoped to find a safe footing in the snow. The summit seemed too far away, too steep and completely pointless to get to, and yet looking toward it inspired a twinge of adrenaline and the thought that he had made it this far.

Then he looked down the mountain, past the snow and the boulder field, and toward the tops of the faraway peaks. There was hardly a hint of them on the horizon, and Thurston knew that there was no medal or glory for him at the summit. The real glory would be returning alive, although sheepish, and seeing a doctor.

The walk back to town was going to be miserable, but it would be considerably worse in the dark. That thought encouraged him to waste no time in getting back down. He took one last look over his shoulder toward the summit and knew that it wasn't the end of his mountaineering career but only the beginning. The summer hadn't yet started, and already he was living a life that he could point to as real and meaningful and not at all like the stuffy academia that all of his friends were stuck in. He said goodbye to the marmot and started down the slope.

With every step, he felt his teeth with his tongue, and it made him feel only really certain of one thing: he really needed to get back to Cañon City and talk to one of those adventurous dentists.

CHAPTER SIXTEEN

AT ONE TIME, THERE WERE FIFTY-FOUR MOUNTAINS ABOVE fourteen thousand feet in Colorado. For the vast majority of them, a steady gait and strong lungs were all the equipment needed to make it to the summit. And people summitted them frequently. Skiers, hikers, gypsies, climbers, commies, racists, hotshots, aliens, Christians, and Buddhists all sought the comfort of the alpine. The tallest among the giants, Bowman Peak, cast a shadow over the entire Idlewild Valley and nestled among the trees at the base of the mountain; somewhere in the Fairy Forest was the illustrious Elk's View Lodge.

The Elk's View Lodge was originally built as the American estate for Cyrus Ames Longjohn, the former envoy to America via Austria and vast collector of an assortment of miniatures. Anything and everything miniaturized fascinated Longjohn. As a boy, his weak disposition kept him bedridden, and due to what Austrian doctors diagnosed as Eselkopf syndrome, written words troubled him. To cope, Cyrus gathered all his resources beside his bed and played on his nightside table.

Little soldiers moved around small cannons and whipped tiny horses. The soldiers spoke in high-pitched, posh British accents. The tiny Austrian soldiers won the battles frequently. That was until the turn of the century when his family moved abroad. They spent time in Sydney and Bombay before finally getting settled in New York City. Throughout the travels, Cyrus collected more and more miniatures. But his fascination with the American West grew alongside his collection. The cowboys and teepees and small horses replaced most of the European stock and were a constant on his bedside table. By the age of thirty-nine, Cyrus decided that it was time to move out of his mother's New York apartment, gather his collection of miniatures, and travel to the real west.

The Idlewild Valley captured Longjohn's attention. The mountains jutted upward and walled in the town and surrounding valley. It reminded him of the valleys of Tyrol, and he loved it. The estate accommodated fifty employees, most of whom were cooks and waiters, but there were also entertainers and on-call actors ready to perform a fake Old West shootout at a moment's notice.

As the years wore on, Cyrus realized that he had forgotten to get married and start a family of his own, and in his despair, he sold the estate and moved back to New York, much to the chagrin of the local economy and workers. The house changed owners throughout the years; each added or changed a bit of it at a time. The Snyder family added cabins. The Watsons added the restaurant and owned it until the mid-1980s when the Haim Corporation bought the estate and the woods that surrounded it.

Slowly, the estate and the cabins and the restaurant grew to become a year-round resort with a pool, a fishing pond, and a high ropes course; a family getaway close to home, or at least that's what the pamphlets claimed. And every spring, the hiring team beefed up the staff to cover the summer season. The hotel thrived off of outcasts who had all but failed in their own lives. Pot heads, under-emotionally developed weirdos, and unattractive harlots congregated at Elk's View in late spring, all eager to start their summer gigs. There were students and other youngsters, but most were lifers, sucked into the abyss of Elk's View, never to be seen outside of the valley again. The lifers spoke as if they were ragtag explorers on the vast expanse of the last frontier and not misfits living within an afternoon's drive to Denver.

On orientation day, Carol faced the summer seasonal staff. Most knew her—it was her sixth year as general manager—and most despised her.

"Hello, my summer Elk. I bet you're all eager to get started." She said to the group.

Jesse, the only returner at this orientation session, leaned over to Emily and whispered, "You're in for a treat." He pulled his beanie over his eyes and proceeded to snore.

"For some of you, this is information that you've heard many times and you're probably thinking, get on already. But some of you are new, and this is a good refresher for everyone.

"First, you chose Elk's View for a reason. We are nestled against the National Park. Adventure awaits, and we, the Haim Corporation and the Elk's View management team, encourage you all to take full advantage of your time here. However, there are rules. We deploy what we like to call the 'Speak up' initiative. What that means is if you see something that feels wrong: Speak up. You hear your roommate talking about wanting to hike Bowman by themselves: Speak up. You hear someone trying to bring drugs onto campus: Speak up. It's really that simple. We have a brochure that outlines the initiative in more depth if you'd like to dig a little deeper."

Emily sat cross-legged and listened intently. This was her

first job after college, and she begged her parents to give her a summer to find herself before finding a real job. She wanted to make a good impression. She wore her best sweater and smiled at everyone that looked her way.

Jesse snored beside her. He wore a ratty Metallica t-shirt and an old pair of skater shoes. He smelled like mushrooms. On Emily's other side was Rudy, a Connecticut-bred college student who was eager to spend the summer somewhere other than his parent's beach house.

"I haven't recognized where I've been since Philadelphia. Have you ever heard of Philadelphia?" Rudy leaned over himself and asked Emily. She ignored him at first until he nudged her and continued. "Philadelphia is just such a great city. You've definitely heard about it."

"Can't say I have." She whispered to him. She hoped that he would shut up, but her lack of Philadelphia knowledge ruffled Rudy.

"You haven't?" Rudy gasped. The group turned toward him and stared. Carol stopped speaking.

"You'll have plenty of time to socialize after the presentation," Carol said. "As far as living arrangements go, there are only three rules you need to remember. One, no drugs or alcohol on the property. Yes, I know it's legal, and some of you are over twenty-one, but it's not my rule; take it up with corporate. Second, no cohabitation. What does that mean, you might ask. No boys and girls in the same room with the door closed. Again, take it up with corporate. Third and finally, we are in bear country; please keep all doors to the outside closed at all times and properly dispose of food waste. Do you have any questions?"

"My dad asked if the Meeker secession happens if he'll still be able to visit?" A voice called out from the back.

The late spring snow piled high outside, and the windows

to the lobby glowed blue. Thurston tramped down the road. It had been weeks since he left Cañon City, and he hoped this was the last spring snowstorm. All the time on the high mountain roads had changed his body. His back and shoulders were rounded, but his legs and chest filled out. The walk hardened his face. The acne and uncertainty were replaced with apathy. His days were blurred sunrises and long, winding highways.

The higher he went into the mountains, the less he recognized himself. The nights were frigid, and he wiped frost from his face before continuing onward. The words echoed: he had already come this far and hadn't been gone for very long. Nothing had changed back home, and he hadn't yet changed himself. A real adventure was born out of perseverance.

Thurston trudged onward. He knew that Idlewild was near, but through the trees, the sight of smoke from a chimney caught his eye. He walked down the lane toward the large smokestack. The long dirt driveway butted next to the highway and without clear indication of the hotel, many had driven past and headed right into downtown Idlewild, which planned for such wacky misdirections. One-lane roads fed into one-lane roads, and a quick turnaround was impossible, not without a view of each shop window. The economy perched on a delicate balance.

But after coming down the lane, Thurston walked into the lobby of Elk's View Lodge to see a few guests and Eastern European hotel workers as they ran from room to room with buckets full of cleaning supplies. A middle-aged woman and a young man with long, greasy hair greeted him. "Welcome to Elk's View Lodge," they said together. The woman shot a glance at the grease head, but the boy smiled and turned around, looking over pamphlets.

Thurston straightened himself out. He felt taller, but it could be because his pack wasn't as heavy. "I'm looking for a job." He placed his hands on the counter. His tongue ran along his chipped teeth, and he hoped that they weren't off-putting.

"A job?" she eyed him over; she was eager for him to move so that she could Lysol the counter.

"Yes, ma'am. A friend recommended that I come here. He worked here a few summers back. I'm in school, I've got all my vaccinations, and I'm even house-trained." He smiled a flashy, chipped-tooth smile at the woman. "I walked all the way from the East Coast for this job."

"Sure, you did. Follow me." The woman said. She led him past stuffed deer and elk, and through a hallway adorned with pictures of different viewpoints of Bowman Peak throughout the course of the seasons. "We had a straggler for first-day orientation."

"Welcome, please find a seat," Carol said.

"You can sit here," Rudy yelled. He scooted closer to Emily until his leg touched hers. Emily noticed.

"Hello, everyone," Thurston said. He crisscrossed through the floor sitters until he found himself beside Rudy. "Thanks."

"Any time. I'm Rudy, that's Emily, and the guy sleeping is Jesse. We're both new." Rudy said and motioned toward himself and Emily. "Jesse's been around."

"To continue, the Haim Corporation and Elk's View Lodge management do not agree with the current political stance that some in the town of Idlewild seem to hold. We also do not condone any actions taken by employees in support of the Meeker state initiative. Tell your dad not to worry. I hope that answers your question." Carol said. "You'll each find your room assignment in your welcome packet. If you have any questions, please meet me at the front."

"Oh, sweet. I'm in the Rabbit Dorm. That's the long one right next to the cafeteria. Score." Rudy said. He pushed his mop hair behind his ears and waved his welcome packet around. "Anyone else in that dorm? Catch you guys later." He said to his floor-sitting friends.

"I'm Thurston." Emily turned toward him. Her blond hair and sweater fascinated Thurston. He lost himself in her eyes, and his cheeks warmed.

"Emily, but you already knew that thanks to that kid," she said and motioned toward Rudy. Her smile distracted Thurston, and he struggled to think.

"Um, I think I need to talk to that lady about a job. I'm not actually an employee yet." Thurston explained and stood to go talk to Carol.

"Tell her you want to work in maintenance. It's the chillest job here." Jesse said from underneath his beanie.

As Thurston walked toward Carol, he caught a glimpse of Bowman Peak through the window. In just one glimpse of the peak, he imagined an entire existence. He might have a pet yak and spend winters in the Andes and summers in Colorado. He would cart his yak products to farmers' markets and shops. During the Ecuadorian December, he would spend half his time in the mountains and half the time on the beach with Emily, and they would take turns surfing and making love.

"May I help you?" Carol interrupted his daydream.

"Yes, I actually don't work here." Thurston began.

"Oh my, are you a guest?"

"Not really. I was recommended to apply here, and I've walked a long way for a job. That guy said you might need someone in maintenance." Thurston said and pointed toward Jesse. He hoped that he had charmed her. The view of Bowman was still in sight, and he tried not to fall back into the daydream.

"Well, that is rather unusual. We do have an opening in maintenance. How soon can you start?" Carol asked. The bum in front of her smelled. Thurston looked ragged, and the clothes hung from him.

"I can start as soon as possible," Thurston said.

"Great, here's your welcome packet."

Thurston thanked her and began to wonder about the duties of hotel maintenance staff.

CHAPTER SEVENTEEN

Outside, the snow drifted higher on the roadway until the pass was closed. Thurston thanked every road god that he had arrived somewhere warm and safe before the snow fell. He paced the lobby and stared out toward Bowman Peak. The east face loomed above a boulder field and a small tairn. The trail to the base of the large granite face crossed streams and cut through the dark Fairy Forest. Local legends about witches and sprites abounded. Legend says they whisper secrets to hunters and prospectors that lead them far off the trail to bring extra food to appease them.

The mountain was illuminated in the snow. The deep crags and outcroppings were highlighted by the white, and Thurston traced his eye high over the ridge and followed it to the top. In his mind, mountaineering came naturally, and ice axes and stiff whiskey were the only necessities to make it to the summit.

"Did you start working yet?" Emily said and sipped at her latte. Thurston wore a long black duster, fingerless gloves, knit hat, and high-top Converse All Stars. His beard hung unkempt and stringy. Small wisps of bangs jutted out from under his hat.

Thurston jumped from the interaction. His eyes remained transfixed on the mountain. "Well, fortunately, the snow has delayed a lot of the maintenance projects," he said and looked toward Emily. Emily smiled at him. His heart raced. His head went back to the idea of them as bundled-up alpine shepherds, lovestruck somewhere in the high country.

"Well, I found a nice chair by the fireplace. I've needed motivation to finish The Shining. It's a little long. But today's the perfect day for it." Emily said. She walked toward her spot and stopped and turned back toward him. "A group of us are going to hang out and play board games later. If you want to join." She tipped her coffee toward him, as a wave goodbye, and buried her head deep in the book.

The darkness of the world and the long weeks on the road with nights spent in cow patty fields and the mornings of a heavy hard-to-breath chest were paved over with the opportunity that Thurston couldn't quite place. He stared at Bowman Peak and felt a rush, then he thought about the girl and felt the same rush.

Thurston decided that he would try reading, too. He grabbed a book from the small library in the lobby and propped it up next to a window. He opened it and looked at the words. None of them seemed to seep into his mind. He finally did it. He was adventuring. Maybe he would climb Bowman. Maybe he'd set a record. He was never really athletic, at least not in the traditional sense. But all the walking had helped him get into shape. And he noticed the small signs of abs pushing through his pooch. He stood straighter. His arms were still thin, but he figured that wouldn't cause much of an issue when climbing. There were endless trails all around Elk's View. He wanted to see bighorn sheep and elk, of course, but he really, desperately wanted to see a bear.

"Reading, huh? Isn't it easier to read if you look at the page?" Jesse asked. He smacked the book into Thurston's lap.

"I was just thinking about something," Thurston said. He noted that he was on the first page and closed the book. He would hate to lose his spot.

"She's single," Jesse said.

Thurston looked at him and tried to understand. The man beside him was much smaller than Thurston originally thought, especially now that he was sat up and with his eyes opened. His beanie pulled dangerously close to covering his eyes, his arms and chest were thinner than Thurston's, and he was about half a foot shorter.

"Oh, come on. I noticed you look at her. And frankly, she is pretty cute. A little too cutesy, in my opinion. But you have good taste." Jesse said. He leaned in and spoke in a hushed tone. "But she is a new grad. Not going to stick around here long. Not like us, the true wanderers. Where are you from anyway?"

Rudy collapsed over the couch and rolled onto the floor. He swatted at Jesse and told him to scoot over. "Man, have I missed you guys. The Rabbit Dorm crowd isn't nearly as cool as you all. Are you guys doing some ice-breaking? Well, you already know me but I'm from Connecticut, third year at Babson, go Beavers, and I'm really here to make friends. Your turn?" He said and pointed toward Jesse.

Jesse sighed. "I'm Jesse. I'm an alcoholic. I'm just kidding; we don't drink alcohol here. Right, Carol?" He said loudly, as he looked around for the general manager. "I'm Jesse. This will be my sixth or seventh season. I have worked in all of the departments, and I like long walks on the beach and doing cool shit."

Thurston knew it was his turn. He struggled for a moment to describe his situation. Voluntarily unhoused? A vagabond soul? He decided somewhere in between the truth and what sounded cool. "I dropped out of school to find myself. Left my girlfriend, left my apartment and all the rest of my stuff, and hit the road." He said. He hoped it sounded cool aloud.

"Badass," Rudy said.

"Yeah, badass. So why here? You could have gone to California or Chicago or New York, but you ended up in the most podunk spot in Colorado? Excuse me, tourist trap, podunk spot." Jesse clarified.

"I think I just wanted some adventure. I like climbing and hiking." Thurston said. Both Jesse and Rudy's eyes lit up.

"You climb?" Rudy said. He mimicked climbing movements in the air. "I boulder. My school has a bouldering club. You don't have to try out or anything, but I could definitely still be on the team even if I did have to try out."

"Well, badass adventurer, do you know something we could do tonight that would really show how badass you are? We can break into the Miner's Cabin." Jesse said.

"What's that?"

"It's a cabin on the outskirts of the property. It is a great place to party and bring girls." Jesse explained. A wide grin crept across each of the boys' faces.

The Miner's Cabin was a small, one-room affair. There was no running water, and the nearest bathroom was down the ridge and toward the main lodge. Electricity was limited and lit a single hanging light that swayed with every movement inside. Everyone ducked as they walked around the room. It was drafty and bat-infested and far scarier than anyone imagined it could be. But it was also secluded, outside of Carol's far-seeing gaze, and the floorboards hid booze and weed and old Playboys. It was Neverland, at least for the boys.

Emily, Jesse, and Thurston arrived at the cabin first, and Emily and Thurston weren't sure how to open the door. Thurston looked toward Jesse, he, in turn, looked right back and shrugged. "I asked if you wanted to break in."

"I didn't think you meant actually breaking and entering," Thurston said. The cabin door sat askew in its frame, and the gap was large enough for all types of creatures to squeeze in. "Maybe we can work the door off the frame." Thurston sized the door up and looked for places to hold.

"I'm fucking with you. Here," Jesse said. He handed Thurston the flashlight and pulled a ring of keys out of his backpack. "These are from my maintenance days. Soon, Thurston, you too will be the keeper of the keys."

Emily rolled her eyes, and Jesse opened the door wide.

The group entered the dark room slowly. Emily ducked her head as she entered and fumbled in the dark as she looked for a light switch. "So this is the party cabin," she said. Jesse pulled the string, and a dingy, small light lit up the room.

Thurston looked around. He wasn't keen on being fired his first week, but the idea of having a few beers and complaining about the last six months felt deserved. Three chairs leaned against a table, and Thurston dusted them off. "Hey guys, check this out."

Along the dust-covered counter space, dozens of paw prints danced around. There was no other evidence of the creature, and Emily clasped her hand over her mouth and said, "So cute."

"It's raccoon prints. I'm surprised that more stuff isn't destroyed in here. They will do anything to get into food." Jesse said. He checked the corners of the cabin with his flashlight. "All sorts of little critters get in here. Bats, bears, obviously raccoons, and tons of mice."

"You said bears get in here," Emily asked. She bit at her fingernails and stood near the door. She looked outside toward the lights of the main lodge and wondered how long it would take to run back.

"It's not like they're grizzlies or anything. The last I checked, I think the park has sixty black bears. Not necessarily nothing, but I think there are more black bears in New Jersey than here." Jesse said. He patted the seat next to hers and cracked open a beer. The beer hissed from being jostled during the walk to the cabin. It was warm and frothy.

"I was in the woods for what felt like forever, and I never saw a bear," Thurston said. He reached for a beer. He never really liked drinking beer, and it tasted sour against his lips. "So you've been here for a few years, have you climbed everything around?" Thurston pointed out the window to some of the more obvious crags.

Jesse kicked back in his chair and his boots hit the table with a thud. He took a long drink from his can and let out a belch. "I have climbed everything. And hiked everything. There's not one area of the park or an hour in each direction that I haven't seen. For the first few years, I was competitive and wanted to get everything out of the way, but now there's just not much left to do. That's when you start tying these different peaks together. You can hit Thatch, Blue Bird, Osker, and Ptarmigan Peak in one long day, and then you slide down Ptarmigan Glacier. The kids around here call it T-BOP. Then there's the full circuit, which you can make as grueling and terrible as you want. Technically, it's a long hike, but you bag Bowman, Whittle, Lady May, and Rittendom. To make it even harder, you can start in Boulder, ride your bike a hundred miles, and then start the hike. And Bowman Peak has so many routes that you can make it into a big technical climbing adventure. There are people that try to climb a different route up Bowman every month of the year."

A loud noise came from outside on the cabin's porch. A low, guttural sound pounded toward the open door. Emily backed away from it and stood behind Thurston and Jesse. They both stood and readied themselves for a small room scuffle. The boys' hair stood on end, and their heartbeats pounded hard in their ears.

Thurston walked toward the door. He grabbed a broom and held it tightly. He opened the screen door slowly and planned to jump out and swing at the bear. As he readied himself, Rudy hopped into the doorway and, with his best bear impression, growled. Thurston hit him on top of the head with the broom handle. "Oh shit."

"Ouch. Damn, dude. You were going to kill a bear with a stick?" Rudy said and rubbed his head. Jesse tossed him a beer, and he held it against the spot on his head. "These are warm."

"You're welcome," Jesse said, then turning toward Thurston, he said, "Any time you want to go climbing or hiking, let us know. And maybe keep your stick at home."

Thurston dropped the broom, and the group planned out the next three months of climbing and hiking adventures. Emily couldn't help but stare at Thurston.

The next day, her mind wandered and kept returning to Thurston. He had started to grow on her. Sure, he was strange and unkempt and had a habit of making tasks seem harder than necessary. Oftentimes, he would come into her office with boxes of paper but be unsure of where they needed to go. He carried a toilet down the stairs but hadn't emptied the bowl, so water sloshed out with each step, and he nearly fell. He was also put in charge of the gift shop mannequin repair. Broken arms and legs and disembodied heads surrounded him at all times. Her boss, Carol, was scattered. Emily caught her twice sitting in front of her office window and staring out toward Bowman Peak. She whispered toward the mountain a single word, 'Trout,' and sighed longingly.

Emily recognized that she needed the job and would hold herself accountable to not get sucked in forever. For her, the situation was a job first, living situation second, and time of her life, social club third. And fortunately, none of the boys were much to look at except the strange boy Thurston.

It took a week of work before Carol explained the job to Emily and handed her a job description, which outlined her tasks, the pay rate, and most importantly, how she'd access her email. The voicemail overflowed before she could start each morning, but it was always the same rotation of annoyances. A church group wanted free rooms because they helped troubled teens, the purple hat ladies wanted to host teatime in the lobby twice a week, and weddings upon weddings. She spent hours listening to brides and grooms and bridesmaids and mothers call and explain the importance of the area and the sunset and the porch and that this may be the last time Grandpa will be able to see the mountains. The marriage needed the hotel, and it also needed a chef who would be able to cook Cajun, hand-held foods.

Calls inundated her day, and the emails were constant. The subjects and people were all the same, and every day after work, she sat on the front steps of the dormitory and watched the sunset. The spring sunsets arrived early, and she spent the evenings being thankful that she was able to watch them.

Work overwhelmed her thoughts, so she brought her laptop to her room and made lists of to-do items for the next day, her calendar updated to the fifteen-minute mark. She kept track of every time she needed to interact with a customer or call a caterer.

On her third day of work, she received an email from Onyx Applications, Incorporated, and the stylish headshot of Avery Salis graced the signature line.

Good morning, Emily,

I hope this finds you well. I represent an exciting technology firm based in Ohio and with our next round of funding secured, I'd like to throw an investor's weekend on August 5th,

6th, and 7th. We will schedule a call to discuss catering and room options, but we will need access to a stage for the three days.

Best,

Avery Salis

She read over the email and pulled out a pad of sticky notes when the phone rang. She grabbed a pen and grasped the phone and began writing the dates for Avery's conference when Thurston came in, his janitor uniform was starched stiff, and he carried a large black plastic bag. "Here for litter," Thurston said and bumped his head against the desk as he reached for the trashcan next to it.

"Hello, this is Emily." She said as she answered the phone. She ignored Thurston's head bump.

"Hello, this is Doug Basher with All Paths Lutheran Church in Gail, Indiana. How are you today, miss?" Doug said. His accent was thick and chewed through.

Emily waved her hand in the air to say hello and thank you to Thurston. At the top of the sticky note, she wrote Doug Basher, church guy, and his phone number. Responding, she said, "We'll be reaching out two weeks before the weekend for the deposit and the final head count."

"Bless you. That is just wonderful; please let my cousin, Carol, know that I've called today. May I say a prayer before we get off the phone?" Doug asked.

"Sure," Emily said. She muted the phone and hurried toward Thurston. "Is your head okay? I wasn't trying to ignore you."

Thurston swung the trash bag across his body for dramatic effect. The corner of the desk caught the bag and ripped it through. Apple cores, rotten yogurt, and shredded paper fell out over the floor. "Oh," Thurston gasped and dropped to his knees to reclaim the rubbish.

He muttered apologies over and over as Doug finished the prayer. "In the name of Jesus Christ and the Almighty, Amen."

"Good, thank you. Goodbye, speak soon." Emily hung up the phone and laughed. "You are not allowed in here during office hours ever again." She tossed a pencil at Thurston.

"It is not my fault that they made the corner so sharp. Take it up with the desk manufacturer. That is definitely a hazard. I'll come back and sand it down later. How about tomorrow?" He picked up the ripped bag and held it out in front of himself.

Emily bent over and picked up the pencil and fell into her chair. She brushed her hair back behind her ear. "Have you been up to Needles Point yet?"

Thurston stopped in the doorway again and turned around in small steps. The trash clutched firmly against his chest. "I've gone nowhere since work started. But I'm always down for hiking."

"I'm off at three. I can stop by your room on my way out," she said.

"I'll be there, or I won't be there," Thurston said. He paused and continued, "That's confusing. I'll be there. It sounds fun. Okay, well, I will see you then."

Thurston hadn't thought of Martha since he'd arrived at the lodge.

CHAPTER EIGHTEEN

THURSTON SIGHED. IT HAD BEEN MONTHS SINCE HE LEFT college. Not one sign of worry from reality. Not one postcard, text, call, or telegram from the other side of the country. He left a voicemail for his parents but had never gotten a response. They were busy, he supposed. Even when he was within driving distance, they rarely returned his calls. But none of his classmates or professors emailed him, either, and that made him feel rather forgettable.

Thurston understood that dropping out of mainstream society suddenly and without warning probably jarred the real people. There was no room to blame anyone for not being equipped for such a drastic change. When he left, he never considered that although he was removed from his past it didn't mean that he was uninterested in what people thought.

Emily was a respite from the torment of the past. She was soft and clear and seemed to know how to navigate the complexities of life a little smoother than him. At lunch in the cafeteria, the other employees would talk about rock climbing and skiing and backpacking, and Thurston wanted that. By

God, he should want it; he blew his life apart for that. But then he'd look across the dining room and see Emily. There was no way to be sure, but she seemed not to be interested in the corporate side that the other managers loved. For her, this was a gig and working up Haim Resorts corporate ladder didn't seem to interest her in the slightest.

"Have you hiked the Needles?" He chimed in. The group of adventurers turned to him.

"Oh, yeah. Easy. You follow the road toward the fishing pond, and then it's on the left. You'll see it." Jesse said.

"Be sure to go up before dark," Rudy explained. "Maybe we can tag along with you."

Emily was happy Thurston had agreed to the hike. He was weird and quiet, a tad misguided, but interesting and kind. Everyone else fit together like an ugly jigsaw: the pieces fit, and the puzzle made sense, but there was an over-whelming question of why. Was there nowhere else to go? No friends or family or careers that warranted being else-where. The young guys made sense; they were sowing oats and figuring out the people they were to become. But the single, middle managers that drove to Denver on the week-ends for escape and had nothing else going on, made no sense to her.

The trail made sense. Thurston looked at a map and said, "You just head up."

It wound tight against the fishing pond, just like Rudy said, at the end of the road. It headed into the woods, and Emily followed Thurston closely. His boots looked too large for his frame. It was the first time he had worn shorts since arriving in Colorado. His calves had grown stronger from all the walking, but at his ankles his legs dwindled.

The trail crossed the road and crossed it again. From Elk's View, the houses, cabins, and condos were out of sight and hidden among the trees. But a No Trespassing sign adorned every third tree.

Jesse tapped one of the signs as he passed it. "Thurston, have you ever heard of anarchist squatting?"

Rudy and Emily giggled, and Thurston trudged forward, each footstep a stomp. "No, I haven't." The slope had steepened, and he turned around and flopped onto his bum. His water plopped out of the outside pocket of his backpack and tumbled down the hill. Emily's leg went straight out and stopped the bottle. She shimmied her way from the splits back to a normal standing position and handed Thurston the bottle. He loved the way she moved.

"Anarchist squatting is the idea that these rich fucks can't own everything. I mean, they aren't here half the time anyway." Jesse pounded on his chest. None of the residents of the Needles Point subdivision were full-time. Most were second homes of Denver oil and tech millionaires. "We could have our pick of these houses and just chill. They won't even be here until Memorial Day, and we'll be long gone by then."

Thurston flashed a thumbs up at Emily for the water bottle. "And I'm like that? A reckless rulebreaker?"

Thurston never considered how his current lifestyle choices translated to new acquaintances. For the entirety of his life, he defined himself by not causing a stir, his opinions mild, and, above all else, he avoided confrontation.

But life on the road transformed him into a rogue. Or at least in Jesse's mind. Thurston puckered at the idea of people thinking about him. Thinking about him shitting himself next to the highway or being afraid of being alone or that his teeth were stained and rotten.

"You're the only person I've ever met with so much 'Fuck you' attitude. Like you'd burn down the whole village just to kill a spider." Jesse turned to Rudy and Emily. "You heard why he moved here, right? His girlfriend broke up with him, and this motherfucker dropped out of school and just started walking. That's crazy and impressive."

Thurston nodded. This confirmed his worst suspicions. People did think of him, and it was awful. He preferred when he never did anything and was out of sight, out of mind.

But here sat a group of college-educated, adventurous people that saw Thurston as a dropout and a transient, and they admired him. His rebellious nature was innate. The desire to fit in never stopped for Thurston, he walked from the East Coast to the Rockies and did not come across one place that pacified his spirit.

"You're not wrong," Thurston said. His head hung between his legs. "But the 'fuck you' attitude is hereditary. I got it from my mom."

The group burst out laughing. "This guy," Rudy said, then he patted him on the back and continued upward. The soil fell out from under the ground, and the trees grasped at rock faces and outcroppings. The vegetation thinned, and they could see out over the valley. Jesse motioned for the others to perch themselves on the rocks, and they all watched the sun set in silence.

"This is a great place for a beer," Rudy said.

"All places are a great place for a beer." Emily replied. She pulled out a Red Stripe from her backpack and tossed one to Rudy and another to Thurston. The beer sprayed as they popped open the tabs. There was no room at the top of the mountain for worries.

Thurston used his hands to help himself down the mountain. The adrenaline from exposure tensed his body and his legs spasmed with every step down. "Did anyone bring a headlamp? It's going to get dark soon." Thurston asked.

"I take back what I said. You aren't crazy enough to squat. You're too much of a worry wart." Jesse yelled down.

Thurston remembered his mother and Martha's words. There would never be a time that he would embrace life; life frightened him, and he was petrified by the uncertainty. The houses were obscured by the dense trees. If there were any homeowners, they certainly couldn't see the group. "Pick a house," Thurston said.

The group refused to respond.

"Come on. Pick a house. Maybe we can get in and spend the night. They might have more beer in the fridge," Thurston said. He waited for someone to call his bluff. Courage welled up inside. He felt invincible.

He had gotten this far. While he stood up on a ridge high in the Rockies, the rest of his peers back home were in class studying chemistry. A feeling of superiority and confidence washed over him. "Fine, I'll pick one." He finally said.

"No, no, no. It's my idea. I'll pick the target." Jesse chimed in. His hand shook, and he pointed deep into the woods to a faint glint of glass. "That one. All these years, it's the only house I've ever been jealous of. They have a pair of saunas and a hot tub in the back."

Not a word was spoken. The crew followed Thurston from a distance and watched as he snuck between trees and bushes. The curtains were all drawn, and the garage door was closed. The hot tub cover was firmly in place, and both saunas were locked. Thurston breathed a sigh of relief. These people hadn't summered their summer home yet.

He walked straight up to the front door and gave the knob a gentle shake. Rudy and Emily peered around the tree and watched with bated breath. The door was locked. Jesse placed a cigarette behind his ear and walked in the open toward Thurston. The road was obscured through the trees.

From the vantage point of the house, the Elk View Lodge dormitories were within sight, and Emily noticed. She calculated the distance and planned to trip Rudy if anything out of the ordinary happened, and they had to make a quick escape. She decided that he'd be the sacrificial lamb.

Rudy followed behind Emily. The group gathered on the porch and waited to see the next move. Surely, a rock thrown through a window would suffice.

Thurston moved around the side of the house and tried every window and door on his way. All were locked. The hot tub cover was locked tightly down, and each clasp was fastened from one side. But as Thurston walked around to the other side, a corner clasp was unbuckled and seemed open. Although a night in the hot tub wasn't technically anarchist squatting, he assumed the group would be happy to have a relaxing night, and they could finish the beer. Thurston pulled at the cover and lifted it just enough to notice the empty plastic tub. On one corner, he saw a glint of shine and reached and grabbed it. The key felt cold in his hand, and he replaced the cover and buckled the straps.

"I found something!" Thurston yelled to the group. He ran around to the front of the house and held out his shiny prize. "I found a key." The door opened, and a cold and sterile mountain house awaited.

Rudy found a spot on the bear skin rug and promptly squished himself into the fur. Emily kicked her shoes off and jumped onto the black leather loveseat. Small toe prints were made as she placed her bare feet on the glass coffee table. Thurston smiled at the grand accomplishment. His confidence grew.

The refrigerator was barren. The pantry too. Jesse looked through each cabinet for liquor, or weed, and found nothing. Thurston turned the television on and sat next to Emily. Their thighs touched, and she didn't pull away.

Rudy rolled back and forth on the rug and pulled his shirt

up over his head and wiggled his belly on the floor. "I love this rug," he said. The rug wrapped around him like a human and bear burrito.

The noise of the television blasted through the house. Jesse jumped in the kitchen at the sudden noise. A glass fell to the floor. "Fuck. Will you guys help me clean this up?" Jesse said.

The closet next to the kitchen held a broom and dustpan. Jesse bent over and cleaned up the mess and the rest of the gang sat in different depths of leisure on the couch. He muttered to himself and piled the glass carefully in the dustpan and took it outside to throw out in the woods.

Jesse opened the door with his elbow and held the glass pile against his chest. He gave his mightiest shove and threw it, causing glass to scatter among the trees. Through the trees, a patrol car crawled up the hill. Officer Frank Garcia kept his lights turned off so as not to alert the robbers.

Jesse turned back toward the door and took one step inside. The patrol car brakes squealed, and the officer grimaced as Jesse turned around and looked directly at the car. The cop turned on the red and blue lights and drove toward the house. The hairpin turns slowed the car down, giving Jesse enough time to get back inside. Jesse yelled into the house, "The cops are here." Thurston and Emily jumped from the couch. They clamored over furniture, and Thurston knocked a lamp over. Rudy squealed from being rolled up in the bear skin rug.

Officer Garcia hot-buttoned the outside microphone a few times. The car came to a stop in front of the house. He turned the volume up on the outside speakers. "Hello, I have been informed of a robbery in progress. Please come out so we can talk."

Emily looked toward Jesse for a plan. He shrugged and ran into the back bedroom. Thurston motioned for Rudy and Emily to follow him. They went through the garage. The door rumbled open, and Thurston said, "As soon as it's high enough, we all run in different directions. Don't run straight back to Elk's View."

Rudy gave an enthusiastic thumbs up. A half-hearted smile crept across Emily's face. More glass crashed in the kitchen as Jesse looked one more time for booze. "We have got to get going now!" Thurston yelled into the house.

Jesse barged into the garage with his arms full of champagne glasses. The garage door was open enough for them to get through. "Run!" Thurston yelled. The group made a mad dash through the open door. The champagne glasses fell out of Jesse's hands with a crash. Rudy ran back toward the summit of Needle's Point. Jesse ran straight toward the road and back to the lodge. Sweat poured from Thurston's face.

Officer Garcia watched from his patrol car as the group of lodge employees ran all over the mountain. He muttered under his breath and decided to make one last plea to their decency. "You guys aren't even in trouble. I just want to make sure nothing was stolen," he said over the speaker. A ghoulish-looking kid and a blonde girl ran off toward the canyon. The beanie-wearing one ran down back toward the lodge, and Frank lost sight of where the fourth one ran too.

He radioed to dispatch. "Hey, cancel the alarm. Looking through the house, I think a raccoon or something must've broken in." He sighed, grabbed the broom and dustpan, and began picking up the broken glass.

Emily skidded to a stop next to Thurston. She placed her hand on his shoulder and pulled him close to her. He no longer worried about the dark.

The walk back was quick. Thurston paused at Emily's door and wished her good night. She lingered at the door. He stepped toward her, unsure if she'd invite him to stay. She wished him a good night and promised that they'd hike again soon.

Emily leaned against the wall in the shower. She hoped she hadn't given Thurston the wrong impression. Being single was new to her, and she wondered if Thurston was cute or just there. Was there something about him? Being alone felt heavier outside the city. She wanted somebody, especially if that somebody hiked and loved pizza crust and stargazing.

Doubt crawled out of the drain and followed her to the kitchen. She stood at the kitchen sink and held an empty glass. The doubt jumped into the sink and weaseled its way back into the sewer.

Emily sat on her bed and pulled her legs up to her chest. Her toes were blistered and needed to be painted. She wondered who she'd be painting them for. Her phone sat face down next to her. The bed felt small and uncomfortable. She stood and paced. The night was still young and restless.

She sat in her uncertainty. Thurston was pleasant. His thin, angular face and brash attitude were cute. He was punk and ambitious, in a way, but still very collegiate. He was certainly uneasy. He was young and restless and untethered. Her grandmother would not approve of him. An exciting and harmless affair.

But maybe a summer fling wasn't what she needed. She was nearing thirty, and another boy didn't seem like a good use of time. That was the truth, and she decided to clip the wings of romance where they grew. There would not be a summertime affair, at least certainly not with a smelly vagabond.

CHAPTER NINETEEN

LIFE AT THE LODGE HAD BEGUN TO BORE THURSTON. HE showered often, he ate full meals, and he never considered how he planned to stay warm through the night. With all his newfound freedom, he filled his time by walking. He wandered into town. He searched through shops and looked at dozens of clearance racks. He caught himself in the mirror. He looked healthier. His back straightened, his cheeks were fuller, and he smiled, flashing the row of chipped teeth. There wasn't much he wanted to change about himself.

Even though he felt and looked healthier, a sense of dread filled everything around him. As he wandered aimlessly, he secretly hoped someone would pull him aside and say that he needed to head back home, that his mother had called worried and wanted to hear his voice, or that Martha realized that she had made a mistake. That neither of them called to say they loved him. But no one pulled him aside.

Eventually, even the shops downtown felt redundant. He considered not spending any time at all in the town of Idlewild, that was until he discovered the local bar scene. Pubs filled the dreaded void.

The Golden Eagle was a pub for the townies and locals. Thurston patronized that bar on a weekly basis. He sat in the same barstool, ordered a White Russian, and always said the same weird joke to the bartender, "I like milk." And every day, an old tourist or a lost local pointed to his drink and laughed, and the bartender ignored it.

It had been two weeks since the Needle's Point hike and house break-in, and since then, Emily seemed to be avoiding Thurston. He thought he didn't care. But then he'd catch a glimpse of her as she walked through the employee cafeteria. Or, while mopping, the soap reminded him of how clean she seemed. On days like that, he drank White Russians.

"I don't really know what I did. I flirted with her. I told her jokes, and I was brave in front of her. I showed passion, you know?" Thurston said. He tapped the bar for another frothy drink.

A toothless, leathery local barely hung onto the barstool. He patted Thurston on the back. "Women," he said.

"They are beautiful. But man, they're mean." Thurston said.

Corky eyed Thurston as he sat at the bar. "Hey, I think that's the kid we were supposed to pick up in Denver."

Trout looked over toward Thurston and turned to Corky. "Shut the fuck up. No way it's him."

"No, seriously. What kind of kid dresses like that?" Corky said. Thurston wore a yellow raincoat, his fingerless gloves, and a hunting cap pulled over his ears. "Either it's the same kid, or there are two people that dress like freaks in Colorado."

Trout nodded and thought for a moment. "I know you!" Trout said in a raised voice. Loud enough to be heard across the bar.

Thurston turned and looked at the noise. His heart froze. All the newfound road confidence flitted away as he recognized the large bruiser. He pointed at himself, shrugged, and turned to eye the back exit.

A large hand pounded the bar counter beside him. "I said. I fucking know you."

"I'm new to town. I don't think we would've met." Thurston looked toward the front door and waved to the bartender for relief.

"You know a kid named CJ?" The man yelled at Thurston. It perked up the rest of his crew, and they circled around Thurston's stool. Each seemed stronger than the last, and each sported a scowl.

Thurston failed to understand what had gone wrong. In fact, as far as he could tell, he had done nothing, neither right nor wrong, since he entered the bar. The accusation of his wrongness seemed egregious.

Trout's large hands told the troublesome story of someone born into middle-class existence and only through his own sheer stupidity was brought down to the dredges. "Why didn't you come see us when you got to town? CJ promised you'd be around to help out." The large dumb hands were covered in equally dumb tattoos. The years 1991 and 1992 were etched onto the knuckles and commemorated the back-to-back football state championship wins for Idlewild High School.

Thurston's head was cloudy and filled with mistakes that he made with Emily. Almost as if every word he had ever spoken could have been corrected. He rubbed the crown of his head and wondered if lucidity had escaped him. He could hardly stand from the vodka and heartsickness. He stood unresponsive in front of the goon posse that challenged him. "Get the fuck out of here." His words fell out of his lip and hit the floor.

The gang seemed poised for that reaction. They grabbed Thurston by his arms and legs. The bar stool toppled over, and the bartender and patrons stood amazed at the actions before them. Outside, Thurston was set on the ground. The gravel was wet from the spring runoff. Thurston gulped the cold air. The vodka on his breath did little to warm it, and the air chilled his body. Beyond anything else, he couldn't be sure which was worse, this seemingly terrible situation or the fact that his ass was wet.

"What do you want from me?" Thurston stammered. He clenched gravel in each of his fists.

"Union dues, you stupid fuck." The hands grabbed Thurston by his collar, pulled him up, and he met Trout eye to eye. The posse stood ready to strike. Their knees bent and arms in various fighting postures.

Thurston thought back to the first bully he ever met, Travis Sinclair. The Sinclairs were rich, and Thurston's father consulted them on their taxes, which brought poor Thurston in contact with Travis. As a boy, Thurston's imagination ran wild with all the adventures he would have once he grew up. And he spent most of his time reading. He was content, if nothing else.

Travis and Thurston met at Bring Your Kid to Work Day. Travis wore basketball shorts and braces and had small, brown fuzz sprouting from his upper lip. His dark hair hung in a bowl cut around his head. And without explanation or motive, he walked straight to Thurston and knocked the book he was reading to the ground. It took all the muscles in Thurston's body to stop himself from whining, "Hey!" Instead, he stood and told Travis not to do it again. Unlike the common knowledge that standing up to bullies took the wind out of their sails, Thurston was knocked squarely on his ass as Travis tackled him and pinned his arms to the ground.

The tattooed hands seemed happy to scare Thurston.

There were no union dues for a company of convicts. In fact, they paid no taxes, and most lacked bank accounts. They paid rent with cash and never registered their cars or worried about insurance. Cash was the most important thing to these men, and Thurston had been another body to create more cash.

"I think we should talk to your boss, and this will all be cleared up." Thurston nodded again and again as he said this and hoped it would convince the group.

The thick-necked man gathered himself and wiped gravel from his pants. He considered pummeling Thurston before seeing the boss.

Thurston's heart quickened as the men tossed him in the cab of a large truck. Every word that he wanted to speak, he had enough sense to keep to himself, and the drive was quiet as the truck bounced down the dirt road toward the Medary ranch.

The yard was littered with tractors backhoes, rollers, and large sputtering equipment that Thurston had never seen before. "Nice place," he muttered to himself.

"You'll like Max, he's real friendly." Corky said. Sincerity was all that Corky knew.

Trout grabbed Thurston again and pulled him from the truck. They were certain that this was the right boy, and even if they were wrong, it was much too late for them to admit it.

Max Medary was smaller than Thurston imagined. He stood in the open doorway and didn't quite fill the frame as one would expect. Max seemed large, even though Thurston's eyes could clearly see that he was not. Thurston assumed it was the meanness that made him seem bigger.

Thurston had no reason to believe that Max was mean. As far as he knew, when Max's stepsister's son needed a job, he invited him out with open arms. And when that same step-nephew mentioned a buddy needed a job and help getting to

Colorado, Max sent more than enough money to guarantee a new summer employee. After a month without the new employee's arrival, Max assumed the little scamp took off with his money. And when he realized that he had been in Idlewild the entire time, that pissed him off. It pissed Max off enough that in a moment of impulsive weakness, he wanted Trout to rob Thurston and break his legs.

"Look, kid, I like your tenacity. You walked here from back east? That's a long ass walk, and I know that CJ liked you. I'm sure you're a good guy. But I'm a small business owner, and I invested money to get you out here with the intention of there being some sort of return. Specifically, your labor. So now I'm stuck here with my dick in my hand and short a guy. You see the problem?" Max said.

"For me to not feel like a chump, there are two options: you come work for me for the rest of the season, or we drive you up to Bear Creek and leave you. Even in the middle of July, it snows up there. It's really your choice. What do you think?" Max smiled and nudged at Thurston with his elbow. Max developed a keen sense of judgment from the many years of working outside the norm of niceties. Thurston, scrawny and ragged, was smart, Max could tell. But Max also noticed an overwhelming laziness. It seeped from Thurston. He knew that Thurston would rather sit under a tree all afternoon than do anything at all. A boy so lazy and uncertain that he'd rather walk across the country than face problems.

Thurston's head throbbed. A pink welt formed above his eye. The thought of these tough guys leaving him in the woods did not ease any grief within him. He walked into the woods many times.

There was a slight feeling of regret for not sticking to his word when CJ helped him get to Colorado. Promises never seemed like something that had to be kept. Hope and promises vanished, and no one seemed particularly bothered.

"I'll work for you. I work at the lodge right now, and they provide housing, so I'd need that." Thurston doubted they'd be able to offer housing. A tramp worker, dumpster diving and stealing sleep when he can, doesn't make the best laborer.

If there was any doubt, Max could not show it. This boy stood before him, unlike any of his dumb cousins or the other convicts he employed. The boy knew how to talk and persuade Max, which impressed him. "Fine. You'll work for me on your days off at the lodge. Don't expect to be coddled. This is going to be a brutal summer."

CHAPTER TWENTY

Magnus longed for a large crowd. The green juice worked its way through his system, and he felt reenergized and able-bodied, albeit nauseous.

The theater seemed bigger than Magnus imagined it would be. He had grown accustomed to addressing large groups of people, but this was the first speaking engagement in which the product wasn't the main focus; the attention was on him. He wanted to hide behind the Onyx curtain. If he could point to the application and the way it made the users feel long enough, perhaps they would warm to him. But he wasn't certain.

The back of the theater, behind the curtains, was dark, and Magnus perspired through his shirt. He wanted to talk to the whole crew in the back, but everyone ignored his jokes and jests. The microphone box sat awkwardly against his hip. He worried about his hands, and the sweat formed heavier.

The lights were bright as he walked to the center of the stage. To stage left, Avery stood behind the curtain and gave a thumbs-up. The theater was less than half full, but for Magnus, there seemed to be too many people. He needed a gimmick. He needed to remember the last TED talk he watched and mimic someone more successful. He considered raising his finger, but before he could finalize his plan, the spotlight moved onto him.

"Good evening. You are all here to listen to me pitch myself." Magnus began. The crowd moved around in their seats. In the second row, a man leaned over to his girlfriend and apologized. She crossed her arms in a huff. "I know most of you are here to see the latest innovation to Onyx and probably thought this would be a grand unveiling of a new product. But I am the new product.

"For most of my career, people have wondered if I'm qualified to lead Onyx, but I'm here now to admit that I'm not. I had no idea what it would become. I never imagined that it was going to be a global brand with over two hundred million active users. When I dropped out of school to pursue this, I imagined that it would help get me laid, not that I'd have to appear before Congress."

The crowd settled. The man leaned back to his girlfriend and whispered that this might be interesting still. She uncrossed her arms and placed her head on his shoulder.

"I have no ulterior motives. I am not announcing a candidacy. I will not be running for public office. I am here as an ambassador for change. I want to explain myself and some of the decisions I've made and maybe even make some friends along the way. After today's discussion, I will be in the lobby to answer any questions not addressed during the Q and A portion.

"I want to explain three things about myself today, my three most frequently asked questions: how did I come up with the idea for Onyx, what I do to help innovate the product currently, and what trends do I see in the future? Now, obviously, I won't be giving out the secret sauce, and if anyone, after the talk, wants to work for Onyx, approaching me and handing me your resume is not the best way. This is going to be an honest conversation, and if anyone has any questions during this conversation, please feel free to blurt them out. I will be happy to adjust my presentation."

"Why are you trying to dismantle society?" A voice rose from the crowd. The spotlight shone in Magnus's eyes, and the faces looking back toward him were whitewashed. The green juice rumbled up through his esophagus, and a sudden uneasiness overcame him.

"Excuse me?" Magnus said. The sweat was back. His armpits were drenched, and heat enveloped his head. His heart raced.

The voice stood. "I said, 'why are you trying to dismantle society.' Onyx was cool, and then you started selling the protest data to the police. We have all heard about Portland." The crowd grew restless. Jeers and sneers started as whispers and became louder. There was a rumble in everyone's voice. Magnus wanted to escape behind the curtain, but Avery stood and blocked his way. She motioned to him to continue. Magnus shook his head at her and sweat flew off like a wet dog. "Just do it." She whispered.

Magnus straightened himself and continued. "Portland. Yes, the Portland Riots. Funny that you mention that. It was those riots that led me on this soul quest and this speaking tour. Do you know what the internal Onyx team calls this series? Magnus's likability conferences. I'm here to win back my job at the company I founded. Pretty fucked up, if you think about it. But my likability is linked with Portland."

The crowd settled back down. No one seemed interested in tossing tomatoes... yet.

"The media, and let's just take a moment and relabel them to be a bit more accurate; the clown's den wanted to character-assassinate me. They wanted to paint Onyx as a pro-police, pro-fascist site, and the truth is that we do not believe in infringing on the rights of our user base. Do some of our user base have hateful tendencies? Sure. But I'm sure that racists and hate mongers also use Amazon, and no one is trying to take them down for facilitating Nazis. I digress.

"The Portland Riots were organized by a gang of anarchist squatters. Their intent was to break into high rises and ransack them. Capital should be owned by the people, they claimed. The police suspected that the groups used Onyx to share location information and methods of break-in. I cooperated with the police. That does not make me a Nazi. Any more questions on that? I'd really like to give more detailed information, but as it's still being investigated, I'm not sure how much I can divulge." Magnus paused for a moment. The crowd was quiet. The man who yelled out sat back down and crossed his arms but stayed. No more outbursts to be heard.

"I'd like to explain how I started Onyx, the innovations I oversee, and the future of tech. Which I hope is the reason you all came." The crowd laughed. It was a small laugh. A break from the tension of the Portland Riots.

Magnus loved it. Never before had he experienced in-person reactions to humor. He made another joke and got a bigger laugh. He glanced toward Avery, and she no longer stared at her phone. She gave him a thumbs up and a finger snap.

At the end of the talk, the crowd stood and clapped. They cheered and wanted to hear more from Magnus.

Magnus rushed backstage. He took his microphone off. "Did you see that?" He asked Avery. "They liked me. I think they actually liked me. They didn't like me at first, but then I explained myself and made some jokes, and then they liked me. I never realized what a rush being liked was." His heart raced, and more sweat poured from his face.

"Jesus, you're soaked," Avery said. She grabbed a paper towel from the food table and dabbed at his forehead.

"I was nervous at first, but now I'm exhilarated. It's a sweat of exhilaration. Have you ever sweat from excitement before? I suggest you do it now. Please get excited and sweat so that you can feel the way I do." He waited for Avery to sweat.

"I think I understand the sensation. Are you going to go out and shake hands and kiss people on the forehead?" She asked. An audio technician walked by, and Avery stopped him and handed the sweat-drenched paper towel to him.

"Oh, Avery. That was a lie. We should leave or at least go back to my little room and discuss our next steps."

"The green room, sure." Avery said.

"What are the biggest trending stories on Onyx right now?" Magnus asked. He paced back and forth.

"Lead poisoning in a school in Arkansas. Lil Bird released a new single. There's a secession movement in Colorado. The President is giving an address about..." Magnus stopped her from continuing.

"What's the secession movement in Colorado?"

"A group feels that their community is being exploited and wants to build a fence around the county and make people pay to get in. That community is actually booked as one of the stops for your tour. I was hoping to invite some of the Denver area investors to it." Avery said.

"It sounds like it could be my redemption for Portland." Magnus mused. He shook his head back and forth for a few moments. "We should promote it on the front page of Onyx. I want everyone to know that I care about the plight of the average American."

"Of course, sir."

CHAPTER TWENTY-ONE

THE CREW BOUNCED ACROSS THE DIRT ROAD AND HEADED down the valley. The truck's engine struggled to turn over in the early morning. It cranked and fought and finally sputtered and roared into life. White smoke poured out from the exhaust, and the smell of burning oil disrupted the morning's coffee. Thurston rubbed his eyes. He worked a late shift at the lodge and hadn't had breakfast. The valley lay on the leeward side of Mount Bowman, and the fields were dry and dusty. Each ranch seemed to extend onward for miles, with only cattle guards breaking the endless fence line. Thurston grabbed the door handle. His knuckles turned white from the uncertainty of the day.

Max turned the wheel sharp to the left, and Thurston grabbed on tighter. The truck lurched as it made the sweeping left turn, and the men inside all jostled back and forth as they tried to correct themselves. A smile crept across Max's face. "Boys, do you know what we're doing today?" He asked.

Thurston realized that he wasn't alone in having no idea

what they were doing. Trout gave a half-enthusiastic shrug. Corky, ever looking for approval, said, "Uh, fixing a deck?"

Max's face contorted into a full-on grin. His eyes darted back and forth. His left arm dangled out the window and moved up and down with the shifting air. "We are finding some votes today."

Corky gave out an excited squeal. Trout clapped his hand upon his leg with a thud. Thurston stared out the window. "What does that mean?" Thurston asked.

The truck was silent. It lurched to the right as Max veered into the property where the votes could be found.

"Do we have to explain everything to you?" Max said. The truck came to a halt in front of an old farmhouse. A rickety barn and barbed wire kept the horses and goats fenced in. The screen door on the old house swung open and slammed close every few seconds with the wind. The valley on this side of the mountain differed greatly from the valley the National Park and Idlewild sat. Instead of green, billowing grass and thick trees, it was a desolate sage sea. Everything, including the grass, barn, house, and horses, was the same dusty brown.

"Hang back with me", Max said. He motioned for Trout and Corky to get out. Trout was the first to the door. His large shoulders dwarfed the small farmhouse. His apathy in the truck faded as a strange grimace came upon his face. As the uncaring man turned into a brute, Thurston trembled. He had never witnessed a shift in physicality so vividly. His chest seemed to puff out further. He looked taller than he already stood. On the other hand, Corky had found a piece of glass on the ground that he held very closely to his face to get a good look at. "What do you think of this?" He said to Trout, and he outheld his hand.

Trout ignored him and pounded his large fist on the door. "What do you mean find votes?"

Max pointed to the two men outside the farmhouse but said nothing. Thurston felt his heart in his throat.

A portly man with an eyepatch opened the door. Trout said something, but Thurston couldn't make it out, and then he walloped the man right in the stomach. The tubby man doubled over in pain, and Corky stepped around from behind Trout and smacked him again, this time on the back of the head. The man fell to the ground. A dog came out from around the barn to see what was causing the commotion, but Trout shouted, and he turned right back around to find a hiding spot.

Thurston watched the violence unfold with horror. He was fine with some theft; hell, he was even fine with some light intimidation, but this felt especially egregious. Both Corky and Trout seemed unbothered by the violence. Trout's movements were cold and calculated, although Thurston couldn't wrap his head around what Corky was thinking at that moment. Thurston needed out. He opened the truck door, deaf to Max's protests, and walked straight over to the barn where the horses neighed, and goats bleated for attention. He scooped a few left-over oats from off the ground and held them out to the horse. It was intrigued but wary. The men continued wailing on her master and wanted extra reassurance that she wasn't next.

"You're a good girl... come a little closer. Nothing will happen to you." Thurston said. He stepped through the fence and was within a step of the mare. She let him place his hand on her neck, and Thurston patted lightly and gave her the oats.

"You can't tell her that", Max said. Thurston hadn't noticed Max approaching the fence, but he was only a few feet away. "Something might happen to her. This guy owes me a lot."

"Why?"

"Same reason a lot of people owe me: money. They make a bad investment or a bad bet and, for whatever reason, don't think I'll ever come to collect. Wanna know a little secret? I could give two fucks. In fact, I'm not even here for money. I'm here to stump for the Meeker Movement." Max said.

Max then stepped through the fence himself. He held his hand out and approached carefully, stepping heel to toe so as not to spook the mare. The horse's eye darted from Thurston's to Max and back again, and she pulled away and did a quick trot over to the other side of the corral. "Oh, well. I fucking hate animals anyway."

Trout and Corky called the pair over. Thurston and Max made their way over to the house, stepping through the barbed wire, careful not to get jeans snagged on barbs.

As they drew nearer, the man's face came into full view. His lip was cut and bleeding, and his eye, or at least the visible eye, watered. He had road rash on the side of his face, although as far as Thurston saw, they hadn't dragged him across the pavement. He looked as if he had suffered a rather ghastly motorcycle accident.

"Hi, Rupert. We know you have some feelings about our movement, and I wanted to take a moment to squash any of the misgivings." Max said with a calmness that Thurston had never seen. Usually, he spoke in a staccato, and it was hard for Thurston to make out what exactly was being said. But now, his words and voice felt deliberate and sharp without any room for interpretation.

The man trembled and looked each member of the crew over with his one good eye. The screen door blew open again and slammed shut, startling Thurston. His hands and the back of his neck were damp. He wanted to go back home. He wanted to go hang out in the woods with Emily and never work again with Max. He decided next time that he would make sure that the rest of the jobs he worked were really jobs.

"I understand." The one-eyed man said.

"Next city council meeting, you're going to announce that

your mind's changed. We can always come back to discuss it again if your mind hasn't been changed." Max urged him, each syllable emphasized.

"I understand."

"Great," Max said. He clapped his hands as if to herd Trout and Corky back to the truck. "You've done good work today. Let's leave Mr. Rupert to tend to his livestock."

The men made their way back to the truck when Max stopped and yelled back at the farmhouse. "Oh, Rupert. It's a lovely horse that you have."

Rupert said nothing and watched from the porch as the men drove off his property.

CHAPTER TWENTY-TWO

JAY PARKER WAS AN OCTOGENARIAN, CATTLE RANCHER with no ill will toward anyone. All that Jay insisted was that Max Medary and the crew help rebuild his fence, the fence unbeknownst to Jay, that that same crew had destroyed it to gain access to a rural part of the county to finish their own county-surrounding, new state fence. The fence that Max would charge people to enter through. But Jay couldn't have known that. He was too busy tending to his cattle to worry about the local politics, especially the local politics in such a divisive town as Idlewild.

Trout and Thurston arrived at the ranch early to get started on repairing Jay's fence and to add a bit to the border fence too. Jay wasn't aware of the double goal for the day. He stood outside the tool shed and shook his head.

The shed's shelves were knocked up and down. Paint cans toppled, and mop water soaked the floor. "What happened here?" Trout asked. He picked up debris and set it down. He looked for wire cutters and a post-pounder.

Thurston looked about to see if anything had been stolen,

but it didn't make any sense of what it would have been. The valuable tools sat untouched, but everything around them was wrecked. In the corner, a cooler with sandwiches and hard-boiled eggs had been ripped open and eaten.

Jay sighed and said, "We have a bear around here. Can't seem to get him to take a hint and stay out of our stuff. Ate all our chickens, too."

Trout nodded in sympathy.

"How many bears live in the valley?" Thurston asked. "I saw on the news that a bear around here used to break into cars and eat people's lunch."

Trout guffawed. "There aren't many. Maybe twenty." He said. "Problem bears don't last very long." The pair tossed the barbed wire and post-driver into the bed of the work truck.

The truck bounced down the fence line over rocks and sagebrush. They drove until Trout spotted a downed line and stopped abruptly.

The pair pulled all the gear out and laid it on the ground in front. Thurston tossed the posts out from the bed of the truck. He hopped down and grabbed the post driver. He lifted it high above his head and brought it down hard again and again. The ground was packed and rocky. His triceps shook with each pound. Inch by inch, the post went deeper.

"You aren't too lazy, you know?" Trout continued. "I saw you and thought, what a dweeb. I said to Max I said, 'How is this limp-wristed faggot going to help us?' But just because you're from the East Coast doesn't make you gay."

Thurston stopped and breathed in deep. He nodded his head and agreed. "I'm a little lazy. It never made sense. Work, that is. There was never anything to show for it. I used to work in a store at the mall, and I would bust my ass sometimes. But for what? At least by doing this, I can look down the fence line and see that my day was spent doing something tangible. There is a reason that we're out here. I'm not just scanning coupons for old ladies." The post was finished, and he grabbed the next one. Up and down, inch by inch, it was driven into the ground.

"So you think what we're doing is worthwhile, huh?" Trout wrapped the barbed wire around the post and nailed it into place. "Everyone sells their bodies. We can set the price, sure. But at the end of the day, I'd much rather be in a warm office looking at a computer than out here in the cold swinging hammers. At least those computer yuppies have health insurance."

Thurston noticed movement in the tree line but couldn't quite make it out. "What's the deal with the fence and Meeker Movement stuff? I don't really get it."

Trout took a deep breath and then sighed. "Max is a control freak. He heard all of the 'we'll build a wall and make Mexico pay for it' rhetoric and decided that he thought that the people here were being treated unfairly. It seemed like the locals were being pushed out, and the ones that had jobs were paid like shit, so he decided that a fence around the county with an entrance fee just made sense. We'll see if he sticks with it. He's not one for sticking to plans."

Behind them, there was a loud crash from inside the pickup. Trout and Thurston jumped at the noise. A small, cinnamon-colored bear looked through the windshield at them. He pushed his way into the cooler and tore open their lunch bags. "Holy shit, you were right."

Thurston ran to the pickup and opened the opposite door. He took one of the posts in hand and slammed it against the ground and clapped his hands together. "Get out of here," he called out. The bear lifted his head and backed out of the pickup one paw at a time. Thurston ran to the other side and met the bear as it exited, then chased it while clapping. The bear bounded into the woods.

Trout watched the thin young man yell and thrash at the forest creature. He knew that people would run at bears, but he had never seen anyone do it with such vigor.

"What the fuck was that?" Trout asked.

"A bear." Thurston finished pounding the post in without another word.

CHAPTER TWENTY-THREE

Convincing someone to get down to their skivvies under the guise of safety was a nearly guaranteed seduction. This was a typical courting ritual in good old Idlewild. Needless to say, the town did not lend itself to being a romantic city. There were no meandering cobblestone streets or kitschy little tea shops along a river walk. For most of the locals, a romantic weekend involved a handle of Tito's, a decent amount of mud, and at least one ATV. A rather common come-on was asking if "you want to be checked for ticks," followed by an excessive amount of winks. And then, of course, there would be flushed, embarrassed cheeks and a gentle slap. Every Idlewild man knew the mixture of a glassy alpine lake, a few beers, and the fear of Rocky Mountain tick fever was a recipe for success.

Thurston couldn't bring himself to be so daring with Emily. In fact, dating Martha had done Thurston no favors when it came to confidence or self-assuredness. He lacked the bravado needed to check for ticks. His voice wavered when he spoke to her, even for a moment. He was sure that Emily could sense his clammy palms, and the thought of her recoiling as he touched her didn't help. In a general sense, Thurston was not used to women anymore. There was a gorge between what he thought women wanted, the words he spoke, and the implication conveyed. No amount of thought or carefulness made him less creepy; he knew that. And he also knew the ratty, torn trench coat didn't help either.

Most of the time, Emily didn't seem to mind. He wasn't even entirely sure that she thought he was creepy. Perhaps one woman's creep is another's eccentric beau. At least, that's what he hoped. He knocked at her door and wondered if she'd be in. It had been a week since he had last seen her. The last few days working with the Medary crew had him in a funk. He wasn't sure if he needed to be alone or with her, and both options seemed overwhelming. He knew that a stiff drink would certainly enhance both options, and he began salivating at the thought of heading to the bar for a round of White Russians.

Emily answered the door in a t-shirt and what appeared to be nothing else. The shirt hung to her knees and disguised all of her womanliness. If his eyes lingered, would that seem as if he was interested or double down on the creepiness? It was times like these he wished that Rosemarie would have let him keep her old copies of *Cosmo* as a reference point for matters of sex.

Thurston was sure he'd had sex before. In fact, he knew he had. He'd certainly seen a woman naked before. But none of that previous business seemed to help with the current matter at hand. Because with Emily in front of him at that moment, he was petrified of what to say or do. If he kissed her, would she be receptive? If she knew he was at the door, perhaps this was a not-so-subtle way of saying, 'Come on in, stupid, I've been waiting.' Or perhaps she was waiting for someone else, and a hard slap would be the warranted response.

All of this happened in a matter of seconds, although it was a beat long enough for Emily to notice how uncomfortable and strange Thurston was. He stood in the doorway, not quite mouth agape, eyes darting back and forth from her chest and somewhere down the hall. She was an adult and not incredibly modest. It wasn't the first time a man saw her in a shirt.

"Were we supposed to hang out tonight?" Emily asked.

The words jolted Thurston from his stupor. He shook his head and fixed his eyes on hers, the safest place he could think to look.

"If you give me a minute, I'll get dressed; and we could go for a walk."

Emily closed the door straight in his face. The door was really what jolted him back into reality as it nearly smacked him right in the nose. Thurston fixed his shirt and straightened out his back. Rosemarie's constant badgering about his posture finally stuck as he tried to look as presentable as possible given the circumstances. He still looked like a ghoul—he knew that. But he hoped that he could at least look like a rather tall ghoul.

When the door opened back up, Emily clapped her hands and said, "Let's go."

Emily walked past Thurston without a glance and out the door. She talked to him, and he wasn't quite sure what it was that she said, but he admired it. The words fell out of her mouth with such ferocity and vigor that he was sure that what she was saying was intelligent, and he nodded along for fear of seeming unintelligent.

"Ice cream." Thurston said. It wasn't an appropriate response to the question that Emily posed. But he wasn't even really sure what she said to begin with, and he hoped that bites of ice cream would temper her speech.

"You're weird, but yeah, that's a good idea. Maybe a quick paddle after." She turned toward the general store and began marching to it. "But anyway, where do you stand on the idea that we are headed toward techno-feudalism? I mean, it's clearly evident that that's the direction we're headed. Look at Magnus Levine: a carefully constructed facade of being a goof-ball playboy, when in reality, his company Onyx has suppressed journalists throughout the world. It's really pay to play."

Thurston couldn't wait to get some ice cream to distract her. He thought back to all the pretentious idiots in Martha's circle and desperately tried to patch together a coherent thought reminiscent of their musings. "Well, you know, it's the Global South you really need to be worried about." A sentence Thurston ripped right from Martha.

"Elaborate?"

Luckily, the pair had reached the general store, and Thurston used the door as an opportunity to ignore her question. He had no idea what he was saying, and he wasn't quite sure how to explain to the girl that he said words without knowing their meaning to impress her. Perhaps she'd be impressed by the sheer amount of words he knew. At least, that's what he had hoped.

Rudy stood at the counter and greeted the pair. "Oh, hi, guys. It's a great night for a walk, huh? It really reminds me of walking around campus, the brisk, cool air. Even though it's summer it feels like fall, huh? I'm half expecting my chemistry professor to pop around the corner and ask if I've finished my lab work for the week."

"Hi, Rudy." Emily said. Her presence was enough to make the young man happy. All the developmentally arrested vagabond boys who worked at the lodge couldn't help but develop a crush on a seemingly put-together young woman near their age. She paid taxes. They all paid taxes, but she filed them and was no one's dependent. A real grown woman.

"Just here for some ice cream, and then we might go down to the dock."

"What a great night to get out on the water. My friend Jenna is working the rentals tonight, so make sure to say 'hi' to me. She's actually a really good friend even though I've only known her for a few weeks. Her roommate was a midnight runner. Have you ever heard of that? A midnight runner?"

Thurston waited a moment, hoping that Emily would continue the conversation since she initially engaged in it. But after thirty seconds in silent awkwardness, Thurston said. "No, I haven't. What's that mean?"

"She left in the middle of the night. No call, no show. She didn't even say a word to Jenna. Amazing, huh?"

"Truly."

Emily and Thurston paid for their ice cream and said goodbye to Rudy. They followed a paved path that led from the general store, past the lodge, down a series of steps to the gravel beach of a Colorado mountain lake. A seasonal dock rocked as small whitecaps rolled in with the wind. Next to the dock, a shack with a large sliding window overlooked a stack of canoes and kayaks. Jenna stood at the window and stared at her phone as the pair approached.

"It's too late to rent anything," Jenna said before Thurston or Emily could ask.

"Why are you still working then?" Emily asked. The ice cream in her mouth made her sound like a Muppet as she spoke.

"I have to wait here until the guests all return their rentals."

Emily nodded but silently disagreed. She couldn't think of one good reason that staff members couldn't go out after hours. If they seemed nefarious, certainly, but they both had loads of ice cream and plenty of daylight left for a paddle.

Thurston sensed the tension and decided to speak up. "Rudy, actually said that you would hook us up even though it's after hours. I know it's against the rules, but he said that you might be able to make an exception."

Jenna rolled her eyes but acquiesced.

The cove extended out and was protected by the large Bear Island. For such an insignificant lake, the island was quite substantial; it lay just outside the national forest park boundary, so oversight was minimal. The camping limit was sixteen days, and at the narrowest part of the lake, you could swim to the shore of the grand isle.

Emily sat behind Thurston in the canoe and watched him stroke. His arms wavered with each as he dug at the water and tried to pull them forward as if he were crawling up a collapsing sand dune. "Hey, Thurston. Have you ever canoed before?"

There was a moment of hesitation. He hadn't; that was abundantly clear. But he decided to lie.

"Yeah, loads of times. My parents' house was along a river."

"Huh." The lie didn't convince her. "What did you mean by needing to be worried about the Global South. I think I understand what you meant, but I want to make sure."

She had him. He wasn't entirely sure what all constituted the Global South, and he was even more uncertain in what context tech oligarchs had in their demise. He could guess, but that might make it worse. He stopped paddling. It's very hard for him to think and move at the same time, and the sudden stop in motion helped clear his head for a big, fat lie.

"Just tech companies outsourcing to Australia. It's a big problem."

It was dumb. His confident lie fell flat against the lake. Even he couldn't believe what he said.

"I don't think that you know what you're talking about." Emily said. They were within feet of the island. "When we get to the shore, I might swim back. Since you have so much experience paddling, that won't be a problem for you to get back, right?"

"Not a problem at all."

They pulled up to shore, and Emily finished her ice cream, discarded the trash at the bottom of the canoe, and waved goodbye. "I'll let Jenna know that you'll be back soon." She ran out onto a rock outcrop and dove straight into the water.

Thurston had never paddled on his own before and a nervous knot formed in his throat. Of all the skills he had learned working maintenance and with Max, this was beyond him. Why couldn't she have asked him to rewire a light fixture?

Emily was out of sight quickly against the dark lake water. The wind-driven waves hid any chance of seeing her. He wondered for a moment if he should worry, and then that concern quickly faded, and he worried about himself instead. The island wasn't too far from the mainland, and he was sure he could get back relatively quickly.

He stepped into the middle of the boat carefully, and it rocked side to side. The wind was pushing the waves away toward the mainland. He placed his hands on either side of the frame and slowly lowered into the front seat. He decided to paddle the same way he had on the way to the island: aggressively.

With a mighty shove, off he went across the rollicking lake toward shore. He didn't dare look back, and he was glad that he wasn't fighting the wind.

Before long, the small shack came into view. Then, a little closer, Emily came into view. She stood on the beach with a scowl and her arms folded. And then, before he could make out anything else, the whole world turned. He tumbled out of the canoe into the cold water, and so did everything: the paper wrapper trash from the ice cream cones, his water bottle, and his hat.

The cold from the water shocked the air from his lungs, and he struggled to refill them as he bobbed up and down. The canoe floated beside him just out of reach. Thurston overhead paddled toward it and reached for the line to be able to drag it behind him as he swam. The line was covered in green algae, and the slime-soaked rope slipped through his fingers. The thought of diving back under the water to try and find it irked Thurston, but it was better than explaining to Jenna that her exception cost the lodge one of their canoes. He held his breath and bent at his waist as he kicked further and further down into the dark water.

He glimpsed the shiny glint of the carabiner that was attached to the end of the slimy rope and reached for it. He looped his thumb through the ring and swam back toward the light of day and the breathable world. The carabiner clipped easily into his belt loop, and he focused on the remaining forty yards to shore. Each stroke and kick felt heavy as he couldn't flip the canoe back right side up, and it dragged against the water. The wind had switched and blew parallel to the beach. The waves slapped Thurston in the face the closer he got to the rocky shore.

Finally, his feet felt the hard, rocky bottom of the lake, and he knew he'd be able to walk the rest of the way to shore.

Thurston walked like an infant as he teetered on the precarious rocks. Some of which were covered in the same green algae slime as the canoe's bowline. It took him an additional fifteen minutes to finally reach the shoreline. He collapsed at the water's edge, out of breath. Emily stood over him, arms still folded across her chest, her scowl unchanged.

"Don't ever lie to me again." She said, leaving him on the beach.

CHAPTER TWENTY-FOUR

THE DOG STOOD ON ITS HIND LEGS AND YAPPED. THE PINK cowboy-hatted man was set in his spot on the corner of Broadway and Colfax and waited for the out-of-town buses to pull in. There wasn't much competition on this street, especially this early in the morning. "Anything to help. Would you like a picture? He's friendly. Go ahead and pet him." He went through the rotation with every tourist's arrival to Denver.

Dottie and Anna's bus screeched to a halt. They turned and looked over the group of ladies. "We need to do a headcount before we exit the bus," Anna called out over the loud group of godly women. Pastor Doug pushed his way through the throng and out into the street.

"If you ladies feel up for it, I may leave you for now. I have a few friends I'd like to catch up with in the big city. Let's all meet back here fifteen minutes before the bus leaves for Idlewild." Pastor Doug said. A sly schoolboy grin crept across his face.

There was not a moment to waste in the new city. All the women sat upright and were eager to be left off the bus. "When you hear your name say 'Present.' Barb, Christina M., Christina S." And each name responded with a 'Present' or 'Here.' "We all need to meet back at this bus station no later than one forty-five."

As a defense mechanism, most of the women stayed close together. The suits and bums and the marijuana smell intimidated them. Denver was one hundred thousand times larger than Gail, Indiana, and that meant for every knucklehead and jerk off, there was an additional hundred thousand than they were used to. "It stinks here", Dottie said.

"They must have a bad skunk problem." Anna agreed. The pair wandered into the downtown mall.

"Hey, girls. Where are you coming from?" The pink cowboy said. The dog buried his face into the sequined vest.

"Gail, Indiana." Anna spouted. Dottie smacked her on the arm.

"Don't tell people that." Dottie scolded.

"Ladies, you don't need to worry. I can't make it very far on foot." He slapped his legs. The wheelchair did a quick spin, and the man bowed graciously. "Do you need a guide today? I can tell you where all the action is happening."

"I think we'll be alright," Dottie said and pushed past the wheelchair cowboy. Anna held back and placed a twenty-dollar bill in his cup.

"Bless you, miss." The pink cowboy said.

Anna hurried to catch up with her friend.

The stores overwhelmed Dottie. It had been eleven years since her trip to Indianapolis, and Denver felt like a chaotic twin. Men on bicycles rode on the sidewalks. Kids on skateboards grabbed onto the rail cars. Bums spit out leftover teeth. Women wore less than expected. And everywhere was hot. The sun reflected off the glass high rises and roasted the older ladies where they stood.

"I don't really think I want to wander too far."

At a quarter to two, the pair gathered their cohorts and marched back past the weirdos and hippies and business junkies and stood next to bus number forty-three. The bus groaned and shifted. Smoke poured from underneath. The driver smiled at the women and gave the key a turn with an almost there, almost there turnover. More smoke poured out, and the bus driver stopped turning the ignition and slapped the wheel. "Good golly." He exclaimed.

"What seems to be the matter?" Pastor Doug asked. Each word he said was a little slower than the last. Anna eyed him.

"Well, not sure. Everything seems to be here, but you never can tell. Something might not be, and that's why we're looking." The driver said. He was not a mechanic.

"Okay, we might go check out a few more things while we're stuck here. Can never get enough culture." The pastor gave a handshake to Anna and continued, "Call me if this gets fixed, will you?"

"Sure." Anna said. Her anger was palpable.

Dottie crossed her arms. "What was that all about?"

"The bus is broken, and I think Pastor Doug has been drinking."

"You think so? It doesn't seem fair that we're supposed to sit here and wait."

Anna shrugged. Dottie punched the air. "You are right to be angry. We have been dragged across the country. We could be having tea and playing squash right now between our motivationals, and yet, here we are, hot and stranded in Denver. Of all the godforsaken towns in the United States, we are stuck in a hot, stinky one? All the while, our pastor is out having a ball."

Dottie stood on the bus steps to see the entire group. "Ladies, we are going to the mountains today. No matter if this bus catches on fire, we are leaving now. Anna, hand me your credit card."

Anna reached into her purse and pulled out her wallet, without a thought. She handed her credit card to Dottie.

"Lynette, call a taxi company and tell them we are going to pay them generously to get us to the lodge. Anna, call Doug. Or actually, don't call him; he's the one that got us into this mess in the first place. Bus driver, we demand a refund." Dottie barked. She fanned herself. A group gathered around her and listened; it wasn't often that a strong older lady yelled in downtown Denver.

"We are headed on our vacation. Does everybody get that?" She said.

"Got it," the group responded.

"I'll get the bus going right now, miss." The driver said and radioed the mechanic.

She came down from the step and patted Anna on the back. "I'm sorry about that. I want to make sure that we all have a nice week here."

"I'm glad that you did that. I was worried I was going to have to make a decision. You really don't think I should give Pastor Doug a heads up? I think I just might." Anna said. She pulled out her phone.

"I think that wherever that weasel ended up is exactly where he wants to be." Dottie said.

Across the street, the weasel perused a bookstore. He found a quiet corner and faced the shelves before he took a long pull of Jim Beam. A thin-lipped employee came over to investigate the drunkard but was taken aback when he saw it was a man of the cloth.

"Is everything alright, sir?" The employee asked. His eyes are wide, but a slight smirk spread across his face.

"Just enjoying the city." Pastor Doug said.

CHAPTER TWENTY-FIVE

THE PASTOR REEKED. ANNA SMELLED THE AIR AS HE walked past on the bus toward the bathroom in the back. "He's a booze hound," Anna said. The pastor swayed to-and-fro as the bus navigated the hairpin turns of the canyon. "Look at him. He can't even stand up straight."

"My brother was a drunk. He died of liver disease." An old woman with a white chiffon neck scarf tied neatly around her throat piped. All of the women within earshot nodded along. Her brother was indeed a drunk and a mean one at that. No one liked a mean drunk.

"What are you going to do? A man, even a man of the cloth, is still just a man." Dottie said. "You can't trust 'em." She added with a huff. She stared out the bus window toward the jagged and jutting canyon walls; she crossed her arms and huffed again. "I'm surprised he's made it this far without a drink."

Anna agreed. Her husband, ever the charmer, had a penchant for alcohol, and if he could fall victim to the trap, then perhaps anyone could. "I'm disappointed. That's all. I thought he was a better man than that."

The pastor wobbled back down the aisle and slumped into his chair. His face was red, and he held down a belch. Anna turned around in her seat and asked, "Are you feeling okay?"

The pastor rubbed his bloodshot eyes and said, "Never better." He closed his eyes for a second and held down another belch. "Ever since I was a boy, mountain roads always hurt my stomach. Does anyone mind if I go in the back and lay down for a bit?"

The women sat in silence, and the pastor wobbled again toward the back of the bus. Soon afterward, a snore reverberated through the bus. The sudden noise jolted Anna, and she sat up a little straighter. Her face wrinkled in anger again, but she would not say anything, she promised herself. This was supposed to be her special trip for the women of the congregation, and Pastor Doug had already made it all about himself. But there was no room for her to be negative, especially when the other women looked toward her as a leader.

And then a clink and a clank and another clink hit the grooved walkway between the bench seats, and a rolling sound came to a stop near the front of the bus. At first, Anna and Dottie acknowledged the noise silently to themselves but refused to look down. Then Anna took a little peek, without moving her head, and saw three empty vodka shooters rattling together on the floor. She refused to move another muscle. Her stoic and stern demeanor was noticed, and Dottie looked straight down toward the bottles. Dottie stood up and said, "Of course he did." She pointed toward the shooters and let all the other women know that the pastor was indeed drunk.

"I am very disappointed."

"A man of God."

"He is just a man."

And each woman in the group said her immediate reaction aloud without any filter. It felt cathartic to complain aloud about a man with him within earshot. The snores and vodka gave them the confidence to share their minds.

"I know you love your husbands or, at the very least, their ghosts, but we need to keep in mind one thing: this is a trip for women's fellowship. Yes, he's here as our shepherd, but we are the flock, and we have each other to rely upon. Next time, we know not to let him wander around a city by himself. That's all there is to it." Dottie explained. Half of the women nodded along in agreement. For them, allowing a man to have his vice was the answer. They'd be able to continue the trip as they had, and once they were at the lodge, there would be gaiety, laughter, and a little bit of wine. Perhaps a small allowance for the pastor would allow them to cut loose as well, without fear of judgment from the others.

But Anna couldn't help but stew. She had spent a lot of money on this trip. The relationship between herself, the group, and the church itself was transactional. She paid, and others did what she wanted, and she absolutely did not want to deal with a fall down drunk on her women's retreat. She glared at Dottie. Never before had she hated her with such zeal. She could typically trust Dottie to have her back no matter what. There had never been a real misunderstanding between the two since they reconnected, but this was a bridge too far.

Anna's fists clenched. Her jaw tightened. She wanted to pop Dottie right in the mouth. She closed her eyes and sighed. Even through her tightly closed eyes, she could hear Dottie's justifications for the pastor's drinking. The excuses swayed some of the other women, and that really was too far for Anna. She stood up and didn't sock Dottie. But she did yell.

"Stop the bus!" Anna said loudly over the snoring, the clinking bottles, and the chattering hens. She yelled so loud that the bus driver nearly veered off the road into the river below. The bus slid back into its lane and then off to the shoulder and finally to a complete stop. The driver put the bus in park and opened the door; Anna marched straight off the bus and continued marching toward the row of trees next to the road. She didn't turn around to see if anyone was following her, and she didn't hear anyone calling after her.

There were a few times in her life that pouting didn't get her exactly what she wanted: a traffic ticket in Dayton, Ohio and a failed Calculus exam her sophomore year of college. Every other time, and with every other type of person, husband, friends, acquaintances, her pouting was not only celebrated but rewarded. A sweet treat for a sad girl was what was often said. Even at her advanced age, her bottom lip expressed itself in an exaggerated way, like a spoiled child.

She expected Dottie or one of the other women to chase after her and ask what they could do to correct the situation. Frankly, there was nothing anyone could do. The pastor had irritated her, that was all. And irritation was something that her money should have protected her from. But without someone taking care of things on her behalf, she'd noticed that life was irritating most of the time, even for the upper middle class. People did not care to cater to her nearly as often as she thought they ought to and a lot less than when her husband was alive.

And yet, the further away she went from the bus, the further away she realized that her friends would let her go. Perhaps she'd continue walking all the way to Denver. That would show the whole lot of them. They'd feel rather silly when they arrived at the lodge and realized that she only paid for a deposit and not the entire weekend. Anna was tempted to look over her shoulder and see if the bus had started back or moved at all. She hadn't heard anything, but curiosity grew inside her. The driver may have placed it in neutral and crept out of there, using only gravity to get rolling. She laughed.

They needed to go uphill into the mountains so there would be no way for gravity to get them there.

Her anger began to dissipate as she imagined all the various ways the women could get the bus uphill without starting it. They all may be pushing it. Dottie would obviously need to do most of the heavy lifting. Poor Ruth would have to chase behind with her walker. Or maybe they flagged down a team of Clydesdales to pull them up the hill. She hadn't heard any distinct clop-clopping, but she wasn't listening for it, so it could have happened while she had been fuming a few moments before.

A distinct, heavy, breathless noise came up behind her. It was Dottie. Her body nearly fell into convulsions from the few quickened steps needed to catch up to Anna. "We need you back on the bus," Dottie gasped. Sweat hurried down her brow.

"Oh, I know that. I was mostly making a point." Anna said. She patted Dottie on the arm as she made her way past her and back toward the bus.

"What was the point?" Dottie asked. But Anna kept walking and didn't turn back to answer. "Hey, what was the point?" She said a little louder and trotted again to catch back up with her friend.

CHAPTER TWENTY-SIX

EMILY AVOIDED THURSTON. IT'S STRANGE HOW FICKLE attraction can be. There had been no change to his appearance or attitude, but now the thought of him felt like itchy perspiration across her neck. The problem, the real bummer of the situation, was that he was one of the only crew members with matching days off.

For the last few weeks, that had been okay. Every weekend morning, a work truck came and picked Thurston up, and Emily didn't have to hide and actively avoid him.

No work truck had come on that particular day off, and there he sat across the dining hall, where he picked apart a piece of toast. He seemed to pick up each torn piece and say something to it before it plopped into his mouth.

Instead of the much more appropriate deliberate avoidance, Emily sighed and sat her tray right beside the solemn young man. "How are you this morning? Excited you haven't had to pick up trash today?"

Thurston looked up from his dilapidated toast. "I guess. Do you think I'm adventurous?"

Emily smirked and took a large bite from an apple. Juice dripped out of her mouth as she spoke. "Adventurous? Yes. Foolish? Also, yes. Why do you ask?"

"My ex-girlfriend said that I was boring and lacked any sort of purpose. My mom agreed. All of this was to prove them wrong, but now I'm stuck working two jobs. I'm tired all the time, and there is no adventure in sight. I could've stayed at home and felt this way. At least back home, I had some friends around." He tossed the remnants of the toast back onto the plate. Each piece landed with a sad thud.

"Thurston, I think you're adventurous. I also think you worry too much about what other people think. What adventure do you want? What lights that fire of yours?" Emily stopped eating and held his gaze. The morning light peeked over the Marble Range, and Bowman Peak glowed pink.

Thurston turned toward the shining mountain and motioned toward it. "I guess that. What else is there? It's almost grotesque the way it blocks the entire field of vision. You can't help but look at it and daydream."

Bowman Peak's size and stature was awe-inspiring. Countless technical routes up the mountain required crampons, plans, and strength. The standard route, itself, was no slouch, with over six thousand feet of elevation gain and a constant possibility of death.

"I've never hiked it before, but the kitchen boys did the full circuit. That's Bowman, Whittle, Lady May, and Rittendom all in one day. They said the snow was gone, and the whole thing only took them like twelve hours." Emily said with full knowledge that the kitchen boys went on nightly jogs and Thurston spent most of his evenings with the television. Perhaps Thurston wasn't adventurous but longed to be, she thought to herself. "Not that I'm saying this is the reason to do it, but it would definitely prove your mom and your ex wrong. We could have a big adventure, and I'll even text them pictures to prove it."

In less than a minute, Thurston unfurled his map and laid it on the table before them. For years, he read so many stories of intrepid sailors and mountaineers pushing the limit of human endurance, and it was finally his turn to write a journal of dreams, complete with map excerpts and quotes from other explorers. He'd thought about this moment for so long; the reality felt malleable and floppy as if it would slip between his hands, flail down the road, and escape away in a storm drain.

How often are dreams so small that they die right at birth? Nearly every day. A large dream has the opposite problem. The Leviathan dream consumes and devours every waking thought, much like an addiction, but most aren't told to stop since it seems like passion. Eventually, the giant dream crushes the person. But a middle dream, a dream tangible and there, so real that when it begins to happen, it's hard to remember if it really ever happened at all; that's what Thurston had been searching for. And that was what Bowman Peak promised.

Glaciers carved the broad north face of Bowman and left sheer granite. Three thousand feet of hard technical climbing without much room for mistakes. Thurston's eyes widened at the thought of him and Emily alone on the wall. High above ground without life's normal worries and intensely focused on small movements. Emily looked over the north face in the guidebook. Not one route on that side of the mountain was possible for the duo and she knew that. In fact, there might have been nothing more impossible for the pair. They might as well have planned on landing on the moon.

The next page of the guidebook described the standard route. A boring black and white gloss photograph of two women in ill-fitting shorts beamed as they pointed to 'the stair-well,' the crux of the route. It was a narrow chute with a drop

on one side and the wall on the other and could only be shimmied up, one person at a time.

"We'll have to do the standard route. I don't know how to
rock climb." Emily stated. Thurston picked the map up in his
hands and stared carefully at the contour lines that described
the stairwell. If a rock fell, they'd be like pins at a bowling alley,
especially if they were caught in the middle of the chute.

The decision was easy and obvious. They decided upon the
standard route; there wasn't a chance that Emily would gather
the proper climbing skill overnight, and Thurston, as confident
as he seemed, suffered from a tragic fear of heights.

The wonderful thing about living at a lodge near a
National Park was that management assumed that most
employees were unavailable during their days off. Not just
unavailable but unreachable. The wanderlust of youth dragged
the employees all over the woods and deep into the forest. The
lodge, in its infinite wisdom, provided bagged lunches for its
employees. A peanut butter and raspberry jam sandwich, a
small red apple, a bag of chips, string cheese, and a juice pouch
were going to have to be enough for the arduous climb. Of
course, they also packed two water bottles and two Gatorades
each.

The alpine start woke Thurston from a sleepless night. His
alarm dinged once at 1:30, and he hopped gently out of his
bunk so as to not wake his roommates. He grabbed his boots,
backpack, and head lamp, and tip-toed outside to meet Emily.
"Good morning," he said hushed.

"Is it morning?" Emily yawned and stretched. Her stretch
swung out, and she slammed her arm against the hallway wall.
"Oops, I'm sorry."

Thurston rolled his eyes. "Let's get going. We've got a long
hike ahead of us."

"How long will this take again?"

Thurston shrugged. "Hopefully only twelve hours but maybe a bit more.

"Great."

He drove Emily's car up the trailhead. It was a new moon, and the stars lit the road like streetlamps. The trailhead, even at that hour, was filled with cars. People were quiet and stretched and said their good mornings, but few were ready to tackle the day. A brilliant early morning for the aggressive yuppies from Boulder.

Despite being nearly August, cold air blew up from the valley below. Thurston shivered and zipped his jacket. He made a point to keep his headlamp turned off, but Emily did not, and he was blinded again and again.

And off they went deep into the dark forest. Within five minutes, Thurston wheezed and raised his arm and indicated that he needed to not only slow down but perhaps die for a few moments. "I really didn't think it would be this steep." His lungs burned with each shallow breath. He alternated between his hands placed on his hips and his head as he searched for relief.

"That's alright, we're here really early. If we need to kill a little time, we'll still have plenty." Emily took the break as an opportunity to eat her string cheese. "Hey, I thought you'd been hiking a lot and were in shape?"

"I guess not," Thurston said and sat down in a huff.

Every minute, another group passed. Each group waved, said good morning, and disappeared into the darkness. Thurston breathed deep. His lungs crackled as he inhaled.

The woods meandered up and over a creek. Emily hopped from stone to stone. Her last leap was short, and her foot dropped into the stream. Her boot filled with the ice-cold spring water, and she cursed herself as she removed the boot and poured it out on the trail.

At mile four, the groups had dispersed. The Boulder

yuppies were near the front, the out-of-state fraternity kids in their basketball shoes and hoodies made up the middle, and near the back of the conga line, Thurston and Emily heaved themselves forward. The grade wasn't as steep once they were past the forest and made their way onto the first of a series of ridges. The headlamps dotted the ridgelines as if it were a pilgrimage. It was a voluntary test of faith on the switchbacks of Bowman. The headlamps were useful in the forest, but along the ridge, the stars and residual glow from life made everything a strange gray. Thurston turned his light off and followed Emily's lamp as it bobbed up and down ahead of him.

During the last ice age, glaciers carved deep fjord-like canyons and valleys as the glaciers slowly bulldozed down the mountain. Erratics littered the remaining land, and those poor intrepid hikers pushed onward and up and over one and then up and over another until suddenly they found themselves in a field of large, terrible boulders, each larger and worse than the last.

As he looked toward the ridgeline, all sense of wonder and hope disappeared. Thurston came to realize that the conga line up the mountain had barely moved. Although the parking lot had yet to fill, two hundred and fifty-four eager and summit-hungry hikers rushed the standard route and found themselves exactly where Thurston wanted to avoid, a long, slow-moving queue in the chimney.

"Let's sit and talk this out." He told Emily. She panted in eager agreement.

Thurston sighed and drank a large gulp from his water bottle. "The chimney is a bottleneck. All it will take is one loose rock, and it's a death trap. I think we either head up the northwest side or just stop and admire the sunrise."

Emily had not considered the northwest route. It was a low-rated technical climb but only truly technical for a few exposed moves along a crackling. The rest was no more dangerous than waiting to get pelted in the stairwell. They agreed that they'd head up the stiffer route.

Thurston hadn't had a lot of time for true introspection. As he slugged his way forward, each step heavier than the last, he wondered why he was even there. No one in the world encouraged him to walk across the country and suffer. And what was it that had compelled him to put himself in situations in which he suffered? Every time he gripped reality and stability and the beauty that was routine, he squandered it by running to something else. His ex-girlfriend and mom had been right, he lacked passion and wasn't adventurous. He was scared. He was scared of missing out and scared of being seen a certain way because, for him, he'd rather die on Bowman Peak than admit he didn't like uncertainty. He had no longing to suffer. But yet he did, time after time. And for what? To prove something to a girl that would never think about him again? To prove something to a mother that would never be happy with him no matter the circumstances?

There grew a depression in Thurston's mind as the point of life unraveled somewhere between the rocks and the route. A small climber's path had emerged and brought Emily and him toward the base of what would be considered the technical part of the climb. A steep four-point hike, a small section of true rock climbing, and a long run up a ridge to the summit. Thurston's legs burned for another break or for an explanation of why they had been brought to this place to begin with.

The route followed an obvious crack up the face, and each hand and foot placement felt stable and safe. He cleared his mind of doubt, breathed, made a move, and repeated. Each placement was meticulous and thoughtful; he tested each hand before applying weight, and onward and upward he went. Emily watched his moves and followed. The confidence

Thurston exuded filled her with confidence of her own. Emily looked back to see how far they'd come, and vertigo swept up the ridge. Her foot slipped from the jug, and her shin slid against the rough granite. "Fuck," she yelled. Her shin burned. Thurston looked down from his perch.

"Oh, fuck. Are you okay?" He yelled down.

She took a minute. Emily cried. Why had she decided to do this? What on earth could be at the summit that would make any of this worthwhile? She breathed deep and whispered a quick prayer to herself. She would go to church. She would evangelize anyone she could, as long as she could be led safely off this mountain. "I'm okay. But this really fucking sucks." She yelled up. Thurston laughed.

The last hundred yards was a steep scramble to the summit. The pair crawled next to each other and reached the summit together. The morning sun hadn't quite warmed the rocks at the top, but the pair didn't care; they sprawled themselves across them as if it was a large, king bed.

The summit spanned fifty yards and had no jagged tiptop, just an open boulder field. Thurston looked to the east toward Denver. The sun glared against his gaze, and toward the west were waves upon waves of mountain ranges. Massifs grew and crested, another came right behind it, and Thurston thought about how far he'd come and how much further he could go. There was no end to the adventure, just the end to the day.

CHAPTER TWENTY-SEVEN

THE GROUP OF ROWDY CRIMINALS SURROUNDED THURSTON and were regaled by his tale of near-death and excitement. Although most experienced much more excitement and death-defying in their own days, they humored the boy.

"The rock was the size of a melon and smashed against the slab beside me. It nearly deafened me, like a thunderclap pumped right into my helmet. And then we scrambled a bit and made it to the top." Thurston knew that half of the group would be impressed; a quarter didn't care, and the remaining didn't believe him either way.

"Wait a minute now, you're telling me that you took a girl that you liked and dragged her up Bowman. And you are wondering if she still likes you?" Corky cackled. The group slapped their legs and spit their drinks on the floor. "Man, no wonder you have such a hard time with chicks if that's how you treat 'em."

"Technically, it was her idea to climb," Thurston said.

Corky laughed hard.

Trout waved the men away, and the group dissipated and

got back to work. He grabbed a shovel and motioned for Thurston to follow him.

"We need a trench about three feet wide and three feet deep dug along this fence line. We are going to start putting in the large concrete posts here and replace all this wood. Got it?" Trout handed Thurston the shovel and patted him on the back. "Bowman is hard. I'm proud of you."

"Thanks, Trout. It's not every day that I accomplish something that I've thought about for so long. It's the biggest thing I think I might ever see." Thurston said. He kicked the shovel deep into the dirt. It gave way at first but revealed a layer of hard clay.

Trout gave a thumbs up and then headed back toward the group of men.

As he walked away, Thurston said, "Well, I wanted to get the climb in while I still had some downtime. I have to work at this big conference in a few days. Then the summer is basically over; I guess it's almost time for me to head to the next spot." The ground alternated with each shovelful between the hard clay and soft, broken-up gravel.

Trout stopped walking and turned back toward Thurston. A conference piqued his interest. It'd been years since he had done a job, but this one displayed itself so readily: a group of conference attendees miles from town and outside of cell phone service. The cops wouldn't be contacted until they noticed something was missing, headed into town, and called. The crew would have a built-in head start. "What did you say?" Trout asked and hoped he heard correctly.

"The summer is almost over. I haven't checked with Max, but I'm assuming the Meeker state fence build will be put on hold for the winter." Thurston said. He leaned against the shovel handle.

"No, before that."

"The lodge is holding some kind of conference. Emily told me about it. I guess a bunch of mucky mucks are meeting to listen to another mucky muck tell them how to get rich. I don't really know what to expect." Thurston picked the shovel back up and piled another bit of dirt. The trench was two shovelfuls deep, and Thurston noticed it had already collapsed on itself. He sighed.

"Come with me," Trout said. He motioned for the boy to follow.

"Like now?" Thurston asked. His shovel was filled with a large scoop this time, and he nearly tripped over his dirt pile as he moved with it.

"Now." Trout said.

Thurston dropped the shovel and skipped over the infant trench. He caught up to Trout, who grabbed him by the shoulder and leaned in close to his face. "I want you to tell Max exactly what you just told me. Don't mention a word to anyone else. Then you can finish the trench. Understood?"

"Got it," Thurston responded. He felt nervous coming to Max, and Trout stayed silent. For being such a large man, Trout cowered and shrunk the closer they got to Max as if they were on their way to the principal's office. Thurston truly didn't understand what he had done wrong and was weary of the punishment.

Trout told Thurston to wait outside and that he wanted to introduce Max to the idea first. Thurston didn't understand and kicked rocks beside the office.

Max's office was a single-wide trailer. The curtains were all drawn closed, and the room was dark; Thurston saw the world narrow as the door slammed behind him. Trout slinked toward Max and whispered something in a low, harsh tone. Fuck, fuck, fuck Thurston thought as he closed his eyes and imagined Max's large ringed hand coming down on his head.

"What do you think?" Max said. Max's hand outstretched in a fist and waited to be bumped.

Thurston gently rapped his knuckle against Max's. "What do I think about what?"

"Trout told me your idea. A daytime robbery is ballsy, but it's all about location, and there's nowhere more remote or harder to get to than that spot in the canyon. Bowman just sticks up there and blocks everything and they haven't thought to build a cell tower closer to the lodge. By the time anyone realizes what's happened, we can be past Durango, riding off into the Arizona sun." This was the first time Thurston had seen Max smile. In fact, it was the first time he'd seen Max happy. Giddy and practically bouncing around the office, he placed different hats on and looked in the large mirror that hung beside the door. "How's this one look?" He said with a trucker hat on. "Or how about this one?" with a ten-gallon cowboy hat perched high on the crown of his head. His hand waved away at any attempt at any answer Thurston might have had. "How big will the crew need to be? Any language barriers? Will we need to use sex appeal? Dogs? Trout to push over fences?"

Thurston's hands shook. He wasn't sure what time or place he lived in anymore, and the room spun. Thurston took a large gulping breath and said, "Five guys. Spanish could help. No sex. No dogs. Maybe."

And with that, Thurston had unwittingly and unknowingly deepened his life of crime. Anarchist squatting seemed to make sense, but robbery seemed a lot harder to justify. He'd need to give himself a good reason.

Trout stood next to Max. The pair looked rough and tumble. "How's security in that place? Is it still Will? That fucking piece of shit." Trout cracked his neck. The veins popped with each slow vertebrate crack.

Thurston couldn't think of a way to safely break into the hotel. Obviously, a smash and grab or guns pulled, and intimidation seemed like a foolproof way to be killed by cops, which was unhelpful when the goal was to get away with the money. No, he would need to be quiet and think fully and carefully to pull this off.

Thurston knew that he'd be able to come up with a plan. He had misremembered a study about the large number of high IQs that seem to be found in prisons. What he failed to take note of was that all of these high-IQ prisoners still ended up in prison.

Max and company evaded the law, or at least felonies, for years. And Thurston had countless resources at his disposal: the full series of *The Sopranos*, Max, some college, and an overabundant confidence from the summit of Bowman.

"With you guys backing me? I think we could absolutely pull this off." Thurston said. His hands stilled, and his mind began to clear and focus on the importance of money.

"I think it's your best bet to pay off your remaining debt to me. And I want to make sure my investment is well looked after." Max said. He wheeled his chair over to a filing cabinet. "We will also be providing security on the investment." A key placed in the cabinet door quickly opened, and a small stockpile of ammunition and handguns sat on top of papers.

Thurston's eyes bugged. "I'm so happy that you'll be able to help with this little venture, but I'm not sure guns will need to be involved. I honestly don't know if Trout will even need to be involved. It's a small hotel, and most of the workers are paid less than minimum wage. They won't give a fuck if some of the guest's things go missing." Thurston said. He hoped that the guns were not going to be forced into the plan. "You guys have done a job like this before, right?"

Trout laughed a deep, hearty laugh. He pulled the blinds

shut and looked at Max before he stated, "We don't incriminate ourselves, buddy."

The room fell silent. Thurston's hands began to shake again. The air felt cold and icy yet sweat poured from Thurston's forehead. He reached for a Dixie cup from the water cooler and spilled it before it reached his lips. He smiled.

"That's not what I meant. I just want to make sure that I'm understanding everything before I get a little too in over my head." Thurston said.

"It doesn't seem like you are into our ideas," Max said and patted the filing cabinet. A nervous twinge ran down Thurston's spine. "How about this? Go home and think about it, and whatever you come up with, we'll decide if it's a good idea or a stupid fucking idea."

And the brainstorm had begun almost immediately outside the trailer. Perhaps the crew could dress like security guards for the event, housekeepers, or even attendees of the conference. Maybe Emily could serve as a lookout and help keep the authorities away. They could light a kitchen fire and cause a distraction. Or flood the basement. These thoughts flew into Thurston's mind without the grace of being helpful or making much sense.

CHAPTER TWENTY-EIGHT

On Bowman, Thurston realized that in order to do something big, he must start small. Each step toward a goal, even a single small step, over and over, would lead to the summit or a pile of wallets and jewelry. Both goals, mountain climbing and robbery, seemed to have equal intrinsic value, and Thurston justified theft in his heart. A surly gang encouraging robbery was also motivation, so was working all summer and having nothing to show for it. Despite being broke, Thurston had been able to afford a growing and consistent White Russian habit.

He walked back to the lodge and looked for a small job he could do alone; there was no need to involve anyone, and besides, this would be an exercise in confidence building. All the houses on the walk home seemed to occupy two schools of thought: large, overengineered McMansions much like his parent's house, but stylized with Western flare. Cattle horns hung over the garage, and buck rail fences surrounded the yard for show. The other school of thought being desolate, murder cabins. The type of one-room shack where the tools and screams can't be heard because of the miles of wilderness that surrounded it. Neither seemed like a good option for breaking and entering.

Even the RVs and trailers down the valley that housed the off-site housekeeping and kitchen staff seemed like a great way to get not only his ass kicked but also to have his life ended. So Thurston passed by all his possibilities only to find himself back at Elk's View Lodge without petty theft success.

The lodge welcomed him in. The front desk busily answered phones and rattled off room rates, Bowman's shadow cast a long dark pyramid over the lot, and busybody guests discussed the different types of mold spotted in their respective bathrooms. Through the lodge window, Thurston saw Rudy working in the gift shop; he banged his head along to music that only he could hear. The tall, cherub-faced New Englander eagerly greeted Thurston at the door. "Hey, man!" He said sing-songy. His hair had grown past his ears, and the baseball cap atop his head pushed it out like feathered wings. "Emily told me about the Bowman summit. Great job, man, great job."

Thurston nodded and browsed the candy section. Everything seemed too big for his pocket, and he wasn't sure if he could grab something and hide it behind his back. "It was quite the hike. Did she tell you about the waterfall?" Thruston's distraction backfired as Rudy came from behind the counter and leaned his arms against the shelf. His chin neatly rested on his folded arms.

He blinked two large and slow blinks. "No, I don't think she did, man. What happened?"

Thurston grabbed a candy bar from the shelf. The plan fell into place without a moment of thought, which must be what people mean when they say someone's a natural. Yes, I am a natural-born thief, Thurston thought. I fell into it much the same way I fell into homelessness and fell up to the summit of

Bowman. Every step, even the small ones, seemed to build to something greater, and Thurston wasn't sure if the chocolate in his hand was a step or a leap.

"So you know the fall that feeds into Tairn Lake? Well, somebody tried to climb up the waterfall. I've never seen anything like it. Buckets of blood. Oozing and gushing happened all around." Thurston slipped the bar into his pocket. He used his now burdenless hands to illustrate the body parts and the eruption of blood. The longer he spoke, the more disinterested and disgusted Rudy's face appeared.

Rudy lifted his chin from his arms. And with every euphemism and blood-spewing synonym used, Rudy took a step toward the counter. And then another. His eyes winced as Thurston spoke.

"The bandages piled on, and nothing, not pressure or prayers, stopped the blood from pouring out. Emily laughed at the guy. Really, she did. She said that it served him right trying to go up 'her' mountain. She's not even from here, and she said that. Can you believe the audacity?" And with every one of Rudy's steps closer to the counter, Thurston matched until Rudy was safely behind the counter once again. Thurston decided to push it over the top. "I've got pictures," he said. He reached into his pocket and pulled his phone out.

Rudy covered his eyes with both hands and pleaded with Thurston to stop. He never wished to know and wanted to forget the grisly details.

"Suture self." Thurston chuckled. He took a step toward the door. "Get it? Suture self?" He waved at Rudy and wished him good night. The candy bar was firmly placed in his pants pocket.

Rudy awakened from his disgusted daze and called out, "Oh, hey, man. Don't forget about paying for that candy bar."

Thurston shuddered to think that he had been had. If

Rudy, the sapless sack, could catch him, how would he be able to pull off a robbery in which real detectives with real working brains would be involved?

Thurston slinked over to the counter and pulled out his wallet. "Must've slipped my mind. It's been a really exciting few days."

"Yeah, of course. Happens to the best of us. Do you have any other big climbs planned?" The dumb kid with wide-set eyes and a little too much body hair for his cherub-like face wanted so very badly to be cool like Thurston. Thurston had become increasingly mysterious to the other staff. How exactly had he walked across the country? Why did it seem like he missed nearly every meal and staff event? How could a girl like Emily seem to be interested in him? And how did they make it up to the top of Bowman without training or an ounce of a plan? The whole place openly speculated.

He had fallen apart so carefully and been divorced from his former life for so long that even Thurston was unsure how he pulled any of it off.

"I'll keep you in mind for my next adventure," Thurston lied. There was something sweet about Rudy, and he thought of himself and how if someone had allowed him to follow them around and learn how to be cool, he might not have run away to begin with.

"Great, I think I've got your number. I'll let you know if we go down to the beach or if we go bouldering. You boulder, right? A bunch of us get together every Tuesday and head out toward Bonnet Lake." Rudy continued talking, but Thurston tuned him out.

This was no different than back at college. He changed everything about his life, and he still was the outsider; even if it made him admirable or mysterious, he was still alone. He wondered how many times he needed to learn the same lesson before it would stick. It was as if life wanted him to learn, and yet, he missed the mark over and over. And now another girl hated him, another group of people seemed to be distant, and the only people that continued to talk to him wanted money. Life hadn't changed at all.

Thurston didn't respond to Rudy about bouldering and left the store in a quiet haze. There was no need to turn back.

CHAPTER TWENTY-NINE

THE CAR, THE HUMANS, AND THE ATMOSPHERE ARRIVED AT
Idlewild in a fit of uniform despair. Avery slouched in the
driver's seat, her arm burned red from being propped in the
window, her eyes and face were hot and bloodshot, and her
bladder irritated from the gallons of coffee it took to drive
across the country as Magnus searched for enlightenment and
likability. Magnus rose stiff from having slept against the
window; his body had been contorted with one leg up on the
dashboard while his head and arms smeared across the window
and the other leg neatly tucked under his bum. He groaned,
and an explosive belch came out as the decayed green juice
gurgled from him.

"Glad to hear you're awake now," Avery said. The window
beside Magnus slowly rolled open so that he had time to resus-
citate himself. "In case you were wondering, we've made it to
the hotel."

"I didn't expect fresh air to smell so bad," Magnus said and
rolled the window back up. "Thanks a lot, Avery. Now, the
smell has gotten inside the car. It'll take forever to air out."

The hotel sat hidden among the trees. The drive extended further and further back as the car crept through the forest and bounced on the pits and marks. The crew screeched to a halt in the large parking lot, and the pair moaned as they stepped out of the car. Stretches and yawns echoed against the large bay windows and wooden porch.

"I know I came to a very healthy and good decision to be rid of the green smoothies. But looking at that mountain inspires me. I really ought to try and get in shape for the betterment of myself and the betterment of Onyx. I'll order more smoothies for the drive home." Magnus said. Bowman Peak loomed in mist overhead and Magnus marveled at how the uprising continued into the sky with no real sense of ending. The entirety of the massif filled the southern skyline.

"I'll look into ordering more green smoothies for the trip back," Avery said. She felt her blood pressure rise and motioned for Magnus to follow her to the door.

The lodge seemed artificially quaint and stuffy. The main room was filled with taxidermied animals from the National Park and heavy wood furniture. The check-in desk was a small station with a window. No concierges or doormen, just a short line of receptionists. It was a quiet and delicate operation nestled among the craggy behemoths.

"Avery, please get us checked in. I'll be over here." Magnus motioned toward the mantle and collection of books. The books were decorative, and each row hardcovers in a different color. There was no reason for Fenimore Cooper wilderness tales to be set next to a breastfeeding manual and the history of Lincoln County, Iowa, other than, of course, that each had been bound with a distinct shade of blue.

Magnus watched a barn swallow prance along the porch as if it kept a secret. The little bird with even smaller feet hopped closer and closer to the window, and Magnus couldn't tell if it was him or the bird's own reflection that had drawn it to stare into the window. Then, without any prompting, the bird flew off the porch and didn't stop to look back. "I stared into the darkness, and the darkness stared back," Magnus chuckled. The little bird dared not see the monster in the window again.

Avery tapped Magnus on the shoulder, and he let out a yelp. "I didn't mean to frighten you. I thought you were talking to me." Magnus shrugged and wiped his shoulders off. "I have some bad news. It appears as though your room has been double booked."

Magnus shrugged and wiped his shoulders again. "That's not so bad. I'm sure you'll explain the situation to the other guests, and they'll be more than happy to take another room."

"That's the thing, sir. The other guest is already settled in our room."

Fear rippled across Magnus's face and found itself coming up from his stomach along with more green juice. His heart raced and sweat pooled on his forehead. Every thought came together all at once and fell apart. Magnus gasped for air and threw himself out the front door, racing down the front steps. The little barn swallow recognized the monster from the window and dive-bombed him. "What have I done to deserve this?" He yelped and swatted at the kamikaze swallow.

Avery found him perched next to the car. He kneeled beside it and hugged his knees to his chest. His eyes scanned the sky for the flying, would-be assailant.

"Magnus. There isn't much we can do." Avery said. She knelt beside him, paused, and then placed her hand on his head. It felt like a used mop.

"I never imagined I'd be the one kicked to the curb. Maybe you could go in for me and explain that I really need that room." Magnus said. He grabbed Avery and pulled her close.

Avery stood and held Magnus's hand. She pulled him up,

brushed off his jacket, and looked him in the eyes. There was no attraction for him. His eyes were red from fearful tears, his gums stained from green juice, and his prized hair hung in front of his eyes like the aforementioned wet mop. "I want you to close your eyes and think. Somebody is staying in a suite. The same weekend, we invited investors to discuss the next round of funding and your likeability and job performance. It doesn't seem like a stretch that someone else would want the suite. Especially the someones we hope are at the lodge this weekend. Do you understand what I'm saying?" Avery lied. Each time Magnus ignored or annoyed her over the road trip, she took one person off the potential guest list. After months of annoyances, the guest list would have been in the negative if she could have somehow managed that. She took solace in the fact that the auditorium would be empty when he took the stage.

"If I make a fuss, one of the investors could find out and not want to give me more money." Magnus looked at her through his tearful blood-shot eyes. The dirt from the parking lot caked to his face where the tears had run down.

Magnus had courage. There were reserves in him, and people underestimated how much courage was needed for tasks. He called and made dentist appointments, he knew how to drive a car, and he assumed he could climb a mountain if the opportunity arose. At least, he told himself that as he stared at Bowman Peak and walked back inside the hotel. The hotel's lackluster accommodations were much more obvious to Magnus now that he was willfully blinded by the rustic appeal and quaint decorations. The creature comforts were lacking, the rooms were dated but not in an antique way, and the hotel smelled. He made his way to the desk. "Hello, my name is Magnus Levine. I am of Scandinavian descent, so please excuse my bluntness, but will you allow me to speak to the guests in

the room I booked? I'll need the room number and their names."
Magnus said.

"I've spoken to my manager, sir, and tonight's accommodations will be half off, and you'll have a drink credit for the
entirety of your stay." The grease-haired receptionist said as his
fingers clacked on the keyboard.

Avery looked through her emails. The uncertainty of the
weekend suddenly became very apparent even without
Magnus speaking in front of a crowd. Magnus's face flushed
with frustration.

"That is all fine and well. But I think the people who
booked the room may actually be my guests. I'd like to give
them the old Swedish meatball." He said. The receptionist
stopped his clacking on the keyboard. "They are quite delicious.
Perhaps you'd like one as well." He reached into his day bag.
An odor of lutefisk and meatballs rose from the bag, and the
receptionist gagged.

The greasy youth wrinkled his nose. "Completely under-
standable. Let me just get that room number for you." He
clacked at the keyboard again. "It will be room 112 and is
named the Morrison Room. It's named after Jim. You'll know
when you're there when you get to The Doors."

Magnus stared blankly, and Avery smirked as a consolation.

The Morrison Room was named after the Morrison Formation, which was named after Morrison, Colorado, and named
after George Morrison, a Canadian stonemason who found
fame and wealth from the discovery of smooth, large building
stones pulled from the dinosaur-filled Morrison Formation. Of
course, the room bore little resemblance to the formation, town,
or man, but it did have a large brass tub and a stand-alone fireplace, a small study nook, and a pair of queen beds. Paintings of
Bowman Peak and the rest of the National Park lined the walls.
The falls were painted not once but twice. Each with meticu-

lous sketching of the rock face that lined them. Strange that two separate painters, nearly fifty years apart, decided to sketch the waterfall with the same sense of hurried boredom. The rocks around the falls were created with such care that each crack and rough surface that hotel management chose for their 'rock room.' But there was no mention of dinosaurs, limestone, or the aforementioned George.

Dottie and Anna found the room adequate and did not laugh at the receptionist's 'Doors' joke either. Anna touched the greasy-haired boy on the shoulder and said, "That's alright," after several moments of abject silence, which the boy had hoped would be laughter.

Anna set her large suitcase on the bed. She pulled out four pairs of heels, flats, and a pair of tennis shoes. There were two pairs of elastic-waisted jeans, four blouses, a pair of black slacks, and a church dress with a floral print in the suitcase, too. Dottie eyed her as the pile of clothes on the bed and floor heaped more and more. Dottie sighed and unzipped her small bag. She pulled out a Walt Disney World shirt from 1996, a merino wool sweater, and a white and black striped polo. Dottie put the few items in the dresser drawer and slumped into the chair. The drive from Denver took two hours longer than expected due to frequent and small bathroom breaks along the way.

Dottie kicked her shoes off onto the floor, and a loud knock thudded at the door. She cursed and grabbed at her knee and the chair as she stood. Anna hadn't heard the knock or refused to acknowledge it. The beauty of her advanced age was that it was much easier to ignore most things. And as far as Anna knew, most annoyances tended to resolve themselves.

The man at the door seemed scrawny to Dottie. His hair seemed wet and floppy, much like a dirty mop; he had a goatee and a thin mustache, and a big stupid grin spread across his face. "Hello, my name is Magnus." He said. His moist hand extended for a shake, and Dottie scoffed as she took it.

"Anna!" She yelled into the room. Anna appeared in the doorway with a large, welcoming smile.

"Hello, I must've forgotten one of my bags downstairs. This hotel is so accommodating." Anna grabbed her purse from the bed. The small bag jingled with change and mints as Anna searched for a dollar to thank the bellboy. "All I have are quarters, I'm sorry." She frowned at the moist young man.

"I apologize for the confusion. My associate and I are hosting a little meeting this weekend, and I believe you may have been invited." Magnus's smile widened as he noticed the costume jewelry. To him, anything with a gold sheen spelled riches.

"How accommodating! We are here for the conference. We invited as many people from the community as we could, so it should be a rollicking good time." Anna swayed her hips as she explained the rollick that was hoped to be had. Dottie stared blankly ahead.

"Marvelous," Magnus said. His outstretched hand finally placed back alongside himself, knowing that these women had been so helpful. "I think we should get dinner. I'll see both tonight around 6:30 in the main lobby. I love meeting like-minded visionaries."

Magnus left the meeting with a broad and happy smile. These were investors that he knew he could trust.

Avery met him in the hallway with their luggage. "Our room is this way." She said and motioned with her head. She led him down the hall to an equally decorated room. Large tapestries of fur-covered men, fur that sprouted from their faces and chests, chests covered in pelts and topped with beaver-skinned hats adorned the walls of the Kit Carson Room. The fur-covered men wore it with the assumption that they would then use the fur to protect themselves whilst cultivating more fur and covering themselves in even more fur. It hardly seemed that there would be an end to such madness.

"I've saved the day. And more importantly, the company. Those two beautiful souls seem eager to invest and discuss the vision and really spread the gospel of our company. I feel really good about it all." Magnus threw himself upon the bed and left the luggage to be brought in by Avery. "I will need to rest for tonight's dinner. Please be sure to iron my shirt and pants. And make sure they dry. You know how I hate putting on wet, warm clothes."

"A dinner with investors is a great idea," Avery said. Her eyes widened as she wondered who would be attending the dinner. "And yes, texture is everything," Avery said. She removed the already snoring Magnus's shoes.

CHAPTER THIRTY

IRRITATION DRIBBLED DOWN MAGNUS'S CHIN AND DRIPPED on his shirt. He rolled his eyes and sighed. Avery leaned forward, licked her napkin, and dabbed at his face gently. She patted him on the shoulder.

"Please let me eat this bread in peace." Magnus took a large bite out of the middle of the dinner roll. He had not cut it in half or shredded it; he ate it like an apple.

"I want you to look presentable. They'll be here any minute." Avery said. She hoped to quiet his anxiety, but he nervously twitched with every word of comfort.

Magnus placed his hand on the table, and the glass and silverware rattled. "This is a typical investor power play. They'll wait and wait until we've nearly finished our food and then show up as though nothing's the matter." He finished the roll in another large bite.

The restaurant brimmed with people, more people than seemed possible given the size of the main lodge. Many who came through the park failed to realize that there are no other facilities, albeit Idlewild, for seventy miles. They see the restaurant sign and become overwhelmed with fear that something better may not exist down the road. The line led out the door into the parking lot. Kids smacked each other, bored, while their parents felt the ramifications of acute screen time withdrawals. "We're all bored." The mom said. The dad stared at a spot on the ground for well over a minute, with the utmost desire that it may be something more interesting than just a spot on the ground.

Dottie stared at an ornate rug that hung near the entrance of the hotel restaurant.

"How do they make all of those little guys?"

Anna wasn't near and didn't hear the question. But it bothered Dottie the more she stared at the Turkish artwork.

"Hey, how did they do this?" She gestured to the large wall hanging.

"I think with a loom."

Dottie was satisfied with the answer and made her way toward the table where Anna had already sat down. She bumped into each table as she made her way to her seat.

Magnus spotted the geriatrics as Dottie fumbled toward the table. He looked toward Avery and made a big, exaggerated smile. He hoped it would clear all the irritation from his face. Anna and Dottie excused themselves for being late. Anna unfolded her napkin and placed it gently on her lap. "It is wonderful you were able to make it," Magnus said. He glanced toward Avery and rolled his eyes. "I've ordered appetizers for the table; please help yourselves. A bottle of Cab should be arriving sometime soon."

"That is delightful," Anna said. She opened her purse and ruffled through it. A ten-dollar bill sat on top. She elbowed Dottie and showed her the contents, or rather the lack thereof.

"Oh, geez," Dottie exclaimed.

"Is everything okay?" Magnus asked. The air around the

table dried. Avery glanced toward Magnus and pointed for them to meet in the hallway.

"This one forgot to pack her lunch money, that's all. My Social Security check should have been deposited by now, so I think we will be okay." Dottie gave a thumbs up to the table.

Magnus and Avery locked eyes. "You'll have to excuse me. I think I may have forgotten my wallet as well. Magnus, will you help me look for it?"

"Excuse me, ladies." Magnus followed Avery around the corner into the hall. Dottie and Anna spoke among themselves. This wouldn't be the first time that an obvious financier played coy. "Do you think that they are living off of social security checks?"

"Boy, I hope not. I'm not getting very good vibes from these ladies." Avery said. She pulled her phone from her purse and swiped through her notifications. "If the goal behind you being more likable is to bring money into Onyx, I don't think these are the investors for you."

The pair returned to the table. A large stuffed elk glared down atop them. "Well, ladies, an elk at Elk's View Lodge. Seems fitting. I'd like to get down to brass tacks. What is it that you hope to gain from our meeting?"

Anna sipped her water. Dottie looked at the elk and shrugged. She had seen much bigger elk in Yellowstone. Anna leaned forward and said, "It's all kind of exciting, isn't it? To be here and be able to listen to you speak? I don't think I'm over-stepping by saying that we've all been looking forward to it for quite some time." She nudged Dottie.

"Yes, I've had to listen to all those hens yak about it for months. You'd think we were going to prom." She said.

A grin spread across Magnus's face. "I love to hear it. Having a group receptive to what I have to say has gotten more difficult lately."

"That's what happens when Democrats are in charge, unfortunately," Anna said. "I did vote Democrat when Bill ran, but that was just because he was so cute. Much cuter than the other guy, that is."

"Bush?" Avery asked.

"Ross Perot," Anna explained.

"I am very excited to have you ladies attend the talk. And I hope to see you in the front row." Magnus said. He patted Dottie's leathery hands.

"I would miss it if I could," Dottie said.

"You mean you wouldn't miss it?" Anna said apologetically.

"Yes, I cannot wait to see you ladies again," Magnus said.

CHAPTER THIRTY-ONE

Frank Garcia watched as Max Medary sped by. The pickup bounced up and down as he rushed through the tight canyon road, up and over and around. Frank wouldn't have paid any attention to the speedster had he not caught sight of Corky laid out in the bed of the truck, each hand full of rope and shovels and bailing twine.

Frank sighed as he turned the lights and sirens on and followed Max and the rest of the gang to an empty parking lot. He brushed his hair up underneath his sheriff ball cap and came up to the passenger side of the truck. As he approached, Corky sat up from the bed and said, "Hiya, Frank."

"Hiya, Corky. You doing okay?" Frank asked.

"Oh, of course. I've never been better." Corky said. He let the tools down gently on the bedliner.

Trout rolled the passenger window down. Max leaned across his cousin and yelled out, "I know I was speeding, Frank. Carol called me from the lodge and said they had an emergency, and they needed us to get over there as quickly as possible."

Frank looked in the bed of the truck again. There was Corky, rope, bolt cutters, a torch, and what appeared to be ski masks, all being held down by Corky's sprawled body. He made the most of his arms, legs, and belly. He looked up at Frank and smiled.

"What kind of emergency is happening up at the lodge?" Frank asked. Inside the cab were only the two men, Max and Trout. "And where's the rest of the crew?"

"I gave them the day off. With the weather being the way it is, I can't have them building a fence in this heat." Max said. His eyes shifted back and forth as he talked.

"Sure, I understand. The sun's a killer." Frank said. He paused and walked around the front of the truck and waited for Max to roll the driver's window down. He leaned in the open window. "How about I escort you boys to the lodge? Sirens, lights, the whole bit. I don't want anyone getting in your way, especially with Corky holding supplies down back there."

Trout and Max exchanged glances. "Lead the way," Max said. The patrol car pulled out in front of the truck with lights and sirens on; Corky tapped on the sliding glass. Trout slid the glass open, and Corky pushed his head through the open hole.

"Is Frank helping with the robbery?" Corky asked.

The pickup bounced as it pulled back onto the pavement. "You better hold on to everything back there. We need to make up for lost time." Max said. The truck's tires squealed as he sped to follow the police car.

It was no surprise to Thurston that he arrived first. The air was August crisp. The sun had yet to warm the pavement or the rest of the valley. Bowman sat high above, and Thurston felt like he could reach up and tap the summit. For the first time in his life, he felt like he was exactly where he ought to be. He had climbed Bowman, for chrissake. He met a girl, convinced her to like him, and even lost the girl, but still hadn't lost hope. And after all that, he found his true calling: breaking and entering. The work for the day was tangible and alive, but there were risks with real consequences. There'd be no panic because an item wasn't stocked, or a projector didn't work. His nerves shook with excitement.

He picked clumps of dirt from the side of the building. It hadn't ceased to amaze him how muddy the mountains were. A little bit of moisture and, without fail, a dust storm arrived to line everything with brown clumps. When he was a boy, he would visit his dad's construction sites and play in big piles of dirt. He'd dig trenches and toss clumps of mud overhand to push the imaginary Nazis back. All the while, he yelled anti-German sentiments. His dad's crew laughed at the weird kid yelling Kraut at imaginations.

A police car with sirens flashing approached the parking lot. Thurston looked around for the pickup. He wondered if the cop was here for him. Maybe Rudy decided that the candy bar was a bridge too far, and the anarchist break-in had weighed heavy on his soul. Thurston approached the patrol car with his hands in his pockets, and he saw the yellow, dingy Toyota work truck pull into the parking lot behind the officer. Trout jumped out of the passenger side and yelled toward Corky to toss gear. They laid the ropes, bolt cutters, and tarps out next to the pickup. Max got out of the truck in a fury. "Follow me," he whispered to Thurston.

"Fuck." Thurston said under his breath. He followed Max, and they walked up to the police officer. Thurston recognized his thick black mustache and tired, disappointed look. He hoped that the cop wouldn't recognize him, too.

"Frank, thanks for driving us over here, but we really must get to work," Max said. He knocked on the hood of the car.

Frank stepped out of the car. "Any time, Max. I know we

don't always see eye to eye, but you can depend on me. I hope you know that."

Thurston watched as Max's hands clenched into fists. His knuckles tightened, and the white of the bone pushed through. "I know that, buddy. I don't want to take up any more of your time today."

"As long as I'm helping the people of Meeker County, it's no trouble at all. While I'm here, I may go in and see how things are going this summer. I don't get up to the lodge as often as I used to." Frank said and headed toward the lodge.

"I haven't seen Carol since the town hall. I might pop in before we get to work. You boys go ahead and set up, and I'll be right back." Max said. He made deliberate eye contact with Thurston, then Corky, and finally Trout. Each man winced in turn.

Thurston waited until Officer Garcia was out of earshot. "That's alright, guys. The plan works better with fewer of us. Corky, I want you to go over to the water main in the auxiliary building. You won't have to do much to the pipe since the sprinklers go off easily. It won't work with an actual fire because the sprinklers will shut off after a while. If you loosen the nut where the water comes in, the sprinklers will continue running until someone figures out that they need to tighten it back down."

Thurston paused and let Corky acknowledge the plan. Corky's eyes were glazed over, perhaps from the diesel fumes he inhaled on the ride over to the lodge. With a slow nod, Corky seemed to understand what was being instructed, and Thurston continued, "Trout, you'll stick with me and be the lookout. If anything goes awry the signal is 'my friend from Chicago has arrived'. If we hear that we can meet at the Old Miner cabin, nobody goes back there during the day. Try not to freak out. We can still make this work."

"I might," Corky said. His legs squirmed.

The crew moved into their places. Thurston waited and peered through binoculars and stared at the auxiliary building entrance. Once people started arriving, he knew to wait thirty minutes, then give the signal to start.

In the auxiliary building, Magnus prepared for his speech. He brushed his hair flat back and glued it in place. "I have a great feeling about today. I have not had any green juice, and my guts are much better. I have gone over the notes in my head, and you talked to the receptionist about keeping our room for the week. I think everything is great. We create our own destinies." Magnus stared at himself in the mirror as he spoke. Avery stopped caring and listening. After dinner the night before, she called her grandfather and explained that he was right about Magnus. No amount of effort would transform him into a smart and good businessman.

"Whatever you say, boss." She said while she booked her ticket from Denver to Houston on her phone. She wondered if a taxi would come pick her up or if the hotel offered a shuttle service to the airport.

The auxiliary building was a large field house with a basketball court and a small kitchen. There were private study rooms, and dozens of folding chairs were set up in rows on the court.

Magnus exclaimed as he burst through the double doors. He clapped, and confidence exuded from him. Finally, after all this time, funding was within reach and people would like him again. He'd soon be the darling of business talk shows, and he would lounge around in earned excess. There would be Mai Tais and beautiful bikini-clad women and important calls and jets and drugs and all the little things he longed for without any real access to.

Dottie and Anna were the first to arrive. Thurston watched

through his binoculars. He set up about forty-five chairs. He wasn't sure how many investors really would show up, and he wasn't entirely sure how he'd determine which rooms were theirs, but he did recognize Dottie and Anna from the suite. Perhaps all the mucky-mucks stayed in the suites, he thought to himself. There were half a dozen suites in the hotel, and if they were all doubled up, then that would account for most of the would-be investors.

"So glad you could make it," Magnus said. He raced across the gym to embrace Dottie and Anna.

"Yes. We're fine." Dottie said.

"Happy to see you again." Anna interrupted.

"And you expect that most of your friends will be here?" Magnus asked. He motioned toward the rows of chairs.

The women nodded and took their places along the front row. More and more, the crowd grew, and Magnus paced. This was only the second time that Magnus would present himself without the crutch of the application. This older crowd of investors would be scrupulous about the technology and would call into question his intention. He felt nervous.

Avery disappeared into the crowd. Magnus raced to the bathroom and splashed his face with water from the faucet. The cold water focused him, and he squinted in the mirror.

Corky set himself up in the bathroom with a wrench in hand, ready to cause watery chaos. His radio cracked, and Thurston's voice came through softly. "Corky, Corky. You there?" The soft voice paused. "Over."

Corky set the wrench down and fumbled with The radio. The buttons were small, and he still felt a little confused and lightheaded from breathing in diesel. He held the radio against his mouth and spoke. "Yes, I'm here. Ready to rain?"

"What?" Thurston's voice cracked through the radio. "Over."

"Go ahead and make it rain?" Corky repeated. His short and rapid breath rang loud through the radio.

Trout snatched the radio from Thurston's hand and answered, "Does it sound like we're ready? God damn it."

"Geez," Corky muttered to himself and repositioned the wrench near the sprinkler system.

Thurston went over the quickest way around all the rooms in his head. There would be no room for error, and he was excited. His heart pounded at the thought of the money. He smacked Trout on the back and said, "Let's go."

The crowd gathered inside the auxiliary building, and soft, elderly murmuring filled it. Magnus felt surprised by the crowd's outfit choices. Bonnets and floral dresses with matching gloves, fussed hair, and makeup done, this crowd didn't seem as intimidating as he originally imagined.

Magnus tapped the mic. Feedback filled the room, but most of the crowd had trouble hearing it.

"Good morning, thank you for joining. As you know, I am dedicated to the future. Not just any future but one with innovation, stability, and hopefully large groups of beautiful women." He said. He winked at Anna. The room sat still at his flirtation. "Of course, that's not necessarily a goal, just a benefit."

The crowd shifted. A few placed their Bibles back in their oversized purses. Magnus saw the small stirring. "My company will be able to provide people with..." he paused and looked toward the crowd. Few would give him money, he could tell, and he decided to swing for the fences. "What is it you'd like to see my company do?"

A woman stood and said, "You keep saying company. I came here to find out how I can secure my salvation. My husband died last year, and I can tell that there are fewer years than more. I'd like to know that I've done what I need to and get my affairs in order for eternity." The old lady smoothed her shirt and sat back down.

Magnus thought for a moment. He reached into his memory and thought of Billy Graham and Ted Haggarty. He conjured up fire and brimstone and wanted to tie it to Steve Jobs. He could be the Steve Jobs of damnation.

"How can we be sure of our salvation? And are we sure that we want that certainty? There are those who wish complacency upon you. Those with their coffers out expecting more and more. Those who will tell you that there is nothing to worry about, that you just need blind trust. I am here to tell you that blind trust is not enough where I come from. We must act not only in our self-interest but in the self-preservation of our communities. I would like to invite you to do that with me. Yes, I am asking for money. Yes, my coffers are held out, but I am requesting, not expecting. Unlike other organizations that may promise salvation for cash, I will also be gathering mailing addresses and names to send you back substantial returns. This is not a charity but a business, and I'm in the business of helping my community. Each of your investments will help put my company on the map, and we will readily spread the love to each and every one of you."

Anna stood and grabbed Dottie by the shoulder. "An investment in your tech company? An investment?" She tossed her hymnal into her handbag. "Where is Pastor Doug? He said this was to be a women's fellowship group."

Magnus looked at her wide-eyed. "Who's Doug? You aren't investors?"

"Ugh!" The women all sighed as they made their separate ways out of the field house.

"I am so mad I could burn this hotel to the ground. I'm going to march straight to Pastor Doug for all of this and the bamboozlement that's taken place here. They're paying for our hotel and gas and anything else I can think of." Anna declared.

Anna marched through the lawn toward the lobby, followed by a parade of angry elderly women. Dottie seethed behind her; her hands clenched in fists.

In the suite, Thurston found nothing except prayer requests, knitting needles, and bottles of foot ointment. Thurston heard a noise coming from the yard and looked out the window. A gaggle of geriatrics stomped across the lawn as they headed toward the lobby.

"Something's up. Rain now!" Thurston blurted into the radio.

Corky heard the call on the radio and clicked back to confirm. He sat on the toilet, angry and dejected, as he realized there was no toilet paper. "Fuck, fuck, fuck," he thought to himself. He looked around the stall. The floor was covered in dirt and cobwebs, and he didn't want to crawl through them. He stood carefully and waddled to the next stall, but on his way, he noticed the fire alarm on the wall. "Thank fucking God," he said and pulled it. He waddled toward the stall and shut the door.

The crowd of angry women burst into the lobby. Anna, full of conjured hellfire and a lifetime of exceptional customer service, was irate. "We need to speak to someone this instant." She demanded. Her fingers tapped on the counter.

Carol heard the commotion in the lobby. She excused herself from Officer Garcia and Max and popped out of her office. She caught Emily's eye, the only person at the receptionist's desk, and gave her a thumbs up. Emily forced a smile and pointed to the phone held to her head. Carol closed the office door. "I apologize for that, gentlemen."

"Is everything alright?" Frank asked. Max stirred in his seat.

"You both know how the season goes. Angry August." Carol said, and she made quotation marks with her hands.

Back in the lobby, more women piled in behind Anna. Dottie pushed her way to the front and tapped her fingers on the counter in unison with Anna's still-tapping nails. Emily realized she wouldn't be able to keep them waiting much longer and put the call on hold. She turned toward the women and said, "Hello, how can I help you, lovely ladies?"

"About time," Dottie said.

"We need the room number for Pastor Doug. There seems to be a very big miscommunication. I don't know if he wanted our money or just saw us as a group of helpless old women, but nothing about this morning's talk taught me about the Lord. Our pastor needs to be down here now." Anna said. Emily was surprised that the ladies hadn't called for the lynching of the church elders and the destruction of the lodge and all the surrounding outbuildings.

"Of course. I'll call his room now." Emily said.

In his suite, Doug hung up the phone with Emily. "It sounds like our women's group eagerly awaits our arrival. Are you ready to help these poor women realize the love and salvation of Christ?" He winked at himself in the mirror. The hair of the dog was just enough to give him steady confidence.

In the Morrison suite, the would-be robbers were making discoveries of their own. "Trout, these aren't rich investors. They're old ladies here for an old lady retreat." Thurston said.

Trout turned toward Thurston with a handful of costume jewelry. "I thought most of this felt like plastic." He sat it back down on the bed. After a moment of quiet reflection, Trout looked outside toward the parking lot. "You wouldn't have told Corky to pull the fire alarm, would you?"

"No, the bolt he was supposed to loosen would have just affected the auxiliary building," Thurston explained. Before he could elaborate further, the sprinklers drenched the entire lodge.

The old ladies in the lobby leaped and attempted to shield their perms from the wet. Emily directed them to follow her and led the group outside and onto the lawn. The elevator that Pastor Doug was aboard stopped suddenly. The lights went out, and a red fire alarm flashed. "Well, I'll be." Pastor Doug said.

On the radio, Thurston yelled. "What happened, Corky? We need to get out of here now. Chicago, Chicago, Chicago."

Thurston and Trout hurried down the stairs to the meetup location. They were soaked. As he raced down the stairs, Emily spotted Thurston. "Hey, will you help me direct these people?"

"Of course," Thurston said and shrugged at Trout as if to indicate that he needed to leave. "I'll check the elevators."

Pastor Doug bowed his head and began to pray, stopping as the elevator moved again. The smell of day-old whiskey lingered on his jacket. "Oh, good, the elevator's moving. Nothing can make women angrier than making them wait for a sermon," Pastor Doug said aloud to himself. As the doors opened, Thurston greeted him.

"Hello, sir. The fire alarm has been pulled. In order to be abundantly cautious, please follow me out onto the lawn."

"We were supposed to be holding a women's ministry in the auxiliary building today." Pastor Doug explained.

"Oh, I am well aware. Not every day we have such important people staying at our lodge. I think your group will be waiting for you outside. Right this way." Thurston said.

As the pastor was herded outside, Anna spotted him. She scolded Pastor Doug before he even reached the lawn. "You are paying for our food and lodging, and I expect the cost of this whole event to be refunded to all of us."

"I can't control the sprinklers," Doug said.

"The sprinklers?" Anna lunged for the man but was held back by Dottie.

Thurston bid the group farewell and caught up to Emily. She sat against the outside of the building. Her hair was frazzled, and he could tell she had been crying. Thurston felt like he should want to cry. The entire day was a bust. But, instead, he felt happy and excited.

"Holy fuck. What a mess. Want to get a drink tonight?" Emily asked. She wiped the small remnants of tears from her face.

"There is nothing I'd rather do more," Thurston said.

CHAPTER THIRTY-TWO

CLOUDS BUILT UPON BOWMAN PEAK. THE SKY DARKENED, and the smell of a light mountain rain filled the entire valley. Frank walked around the different groups of angry Christian women and explained that a mistake did not warrant an arrest of their church leadership.

In the commotion, Max found Trout and Corky hiding inside the work truck. "How did it go?" He asked Trout.

"They were all old ladies," Trout said. Max grimaced and started the truck. Corky crawled through the sliding back window and laid down on the tools in the bed.

"At least we've got the vote coming up. You'll be a great Governor." Corky said through the small sliding window into the cab.

Max turned in his seat to face Corky. "After all of this excitement, I realized something: it's easier to rob people than to create a state. Most of the crew can stay and work on the building projects here, and we can move from town to town."

"You got it, boss," Trout and Corky agreed eagerly.

Thurston walked through the lodge. The entire place was

ruined with sprinkler water. The stuffed elk heads and the library were ruined. The lunch buffet was soaked. Every room would need flooring and bedding replaced. Thurston realized that he could rob every guest of every single item they brought in the chaos.

In town, the bar was mostly empty except for Magnus. He sat with his head resting in his hand and gently wept into a glass of whiskey. "I can't believe she left. I thought she believed in me. I thought she believed in the company," he said loudly for everyone at the bar to hear. No one turned to look at him. "I guess it isn't enough to be rich these days. Women expect too much."

As he spoke, the crew walked in. Max overheard the whines. He nudged Trout and said, "I told you it's easier to just rob a sucker. There's one now."

Trout sauntered over to Magnus at the bar. "We had a shit day today too. A good job fell through. But you know, things always turn around. This is my boss, Max Medary."

"Would you be interested in investing in a tech company?" Magnus asked the pair of ruffians. Max, Trout, and Corky looked at each other and nodded in agreement. "That's great news. I have a great opportunity for you."

Thurston arrived at the bar and spotted his construction cohorts. He slipped into a seat next to Corky. "Well, we did it. The plan worked, sort of. At least the distraction part of the plan worked." Thurston laughed at the state of things. "Have you guys ever considered a job in Vegas?"

Corky leaned in and whispered. "See that guy at the bar that's talking to Max. He admitted to us that he runs a tech company. We're going to check him out a little later if you want to come."

"I don't know if I can. I'm meeting a girl here." Thurston said and motioned toward the door. "That one, actually."

As Emily danced in, her eyes brightened, and her smile widened as the glow of the bar lights hit her face. "Hey, stranger." She said and pulled Thurston up. She hugged him and led him to the bar. "Weird day. Weird summer, actually. I don't know if I was in a good headspace this summer to like someone, and I didn't tell you that, and I should have. I think my bad headspace might be ending soon, though."

"Oh, yeah?" Thurston asked.

"Yeah. And maybe we could start doing this a little more often." Emily leaned across the bar stool and kissed him gently on the cheek.

Thurston thought for a moment. "Where will we go next?" He asked. The daydream of South American winters came into his head, but he thought better than to say it aloud.

"We could go anywhere," she said. An answer better than what Thurston could hope for. He excused himself and stepped outside for a breath of fresh air. He pulled out his phone and dialed his mom.

As the phone rang, he wondered what he'd say. Perhaps there was nothing to say at all. He listened to the trill and hoped that she wouldn't answer. And with each additional ring, he wondered why he dialed her at all. He hung up the phone and placed it back into his pocket.

When he took his place back at the bar, Emily turned toward him and asked, "Who were you talking to?"

"No one. I think it was a wrong number." Thurston said.